**Ma broke into loud, heartrending sobs.
"What will become of us?"**

Swiftly Eda wrapped a shawl around her
shoulders and tiptoed past her sobbing mother,
down the steps to the street. Pa had left the
wagon in back of the hotel after unhitching the
oxen.

She peered inside, and suddenly she couldn't
breathe. She couldn't think. Maybe this was
the wrong wagon. Maybe she was mistaken.
But the longer she stared, the more certain she
became. This *was* her family's wagon.

It was completely empty.

Everything, including her irreplaceable journal, had been stolen.

Books by Laurie Lawlor

The Worm Club
How to Survive Third Grade
Addie Across the Prairie
Addie's Long Summer
Addie's Dakota Winter
George on His Own
Gold in the Hills
Little Women *(movie tie-in)*

Heartland series
Come Away with Me
Take to the Sky
Luck Follows Me

American Sisters series
West Along the Wagon Road 1852
A *Titanic* Journey Across the Sea 1912
Voyage to a Free Land 1630
Adventure on the Wilderness Road 1775
Crossing the Colorado Rockies 1864
Down the Río Grande 1829
Horseback on the Boston Post Road 1704
Exploring the Chicago World's Fair 1893
Pacific Odyssey to California 1905

American SISTERS

Crossing the Colorado Rockies

1864

Laurie Lawlor

A MINSTREL® BOOK

Published by POCKET BOOKS
New York   London   Toronto   Sydney   Singapore

This book is a work of fiction. Names, characters, places and incidents are products of the author's imagination or are used fictitiously. Any resemblance to actual events or locales or persons, living or dead, is entirely coincidental.

 A Minstrel Book published by
POCKET BOOKS, a division of Simon & Schuster, Inc.
1230 Avenue of the Americas, New York, NY 10020

ISBN: 0-671-77572-3

First Minstrel Books paperback printing August 2001

10 9 8 7 6 5 4 3 2 1

A MINSTREL BOOK and colophon are registered trademarks of Simon & Schuster, Inc.

Cover illustration by Bruce Wolfe

Printed in the U.S.A.

For Peg, a dear friend
who told me about
the dust in the cracks

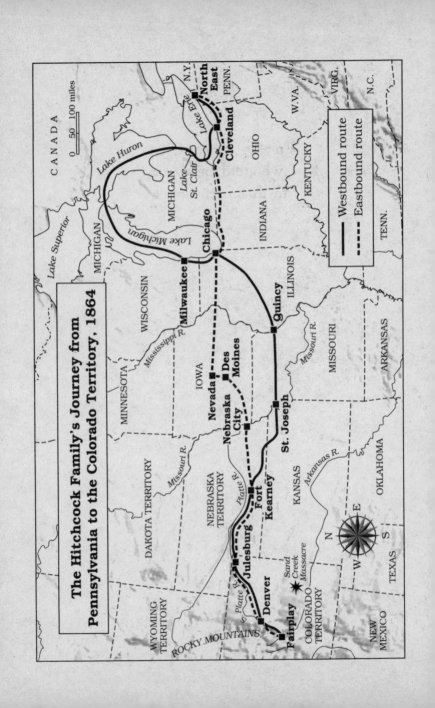

The Hitchcock Family's Journey from Pennsylvania to the Colorado Territory, 1864

CANADA

0 50 100 miles

Lake Superior

Lake Huron

Lake Michigan

Lake St. Clair

Lake Erie

North East

N.Y.

PENN.

Cleveland

W.VA.

VIRG.

N.C.

MICHIGAN

MICHIGAN

OHIO

KENTUCKY

TENN.

WISCONSIN

Milwaukee

Chicago

Quincy

ILLINOIS

INDIANA

MINNESOTA

Mississippi R.

IOWA

Nevada

Des Moines

Nebraska City

Missouri R.

MISSOURI

ARKANSAS

DAKOTA TERRITORY

Missouri R.

St. Joseph

Platte R.

Fort Kearney

NEBRASKA TERRITORY

KANSAS

Arkansas R.

OKLAHOMA

WYOMING TERRITORY

Platte R.

Julesburg

Denver

S. Platte R.

Sand Creek Massacre

N
W   E
S

Fairplay

ROCKY MOUNTAINS

COLORADO TERRITORY

NEW MEXICO

TEXAS

Westbound route
Eastbound route

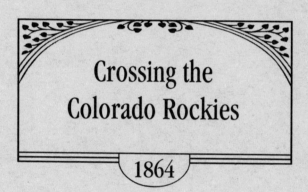

Crossing the
Colorado Rockies

1864

Chapter 1

Eda peered through the opening in the canvas at the back of the wagon. In the yawning valley below, the line of other white-topped wagons looked no bigger than a struggling parade of tiny pale bugs. She hunched forward and scribbled secret code into the journal in her lap:

Woh raf seod a nogaw llaf erofeb ti sehsams ot stib?

Translated, this meant:

How far does a wagon fall before it smashes to bits?

"Get out and push, Eda!" her sister Belle shouted.

Eda tapped her pencil on her knee, stalling for time. "Harriet Adelle Hitchcock." Ma paused, out of breath from using Eda's full name. "We're all walking. You walk, too."

"What about Lucy?" Eda whined.

Her oldest sister gave her a glare that meant trouble. Lucy, who seemed impossibly ancient at age twenty, sat ramrod straight inside the wagon beside Ma's precious melodeon. The pump organ was shrouded with canvas and trussed with ropes. Lucy's pale folded hands gave the impression that she was seated on a hard pew at church rather than in a wagon balanced precariously on the edge of a cliff.

"You know Lucy can't get out and push!" Belle roared.

Eda avoided Lucy's hawklike eyes and wrote:

Belle does not sound one bit like the sweet selfless maiden everyone admires so much at home. Rolling bandages, knitting socks for soldiers. A seventeen-year-old saint.

"Eda!" Pa boomed. "You may be the youngest, but you're adding weight."

Eda scowled. She didn't like to be reminded that she was the youngest. Was it her fault that she was thirteen and everyone else was older and seemed to live in a different, and larger, world? Her sisters and parents worked together to make her life miserable. It was so unfair. She sighed, closed the journal, and slipped it into her dress pocket. There was no escape now that Pa was angry, too. She had to get out.

Lucy snickered. "Spoiled brat-baby."

Eda smiled angelically, not wishing to give Lucy the slightest hint of how she seethed with anger and terror. She gripped the back of the wagon and lowered herself to the ground, knees shaking. She tried not to think about her nightmares. She tried not to think about the drawings in *Frank Leslie's Illustrated Newspaper*, which had made the impossibly narrow tip of Pikes Peak look no bigger than a pen mark. What would happen if her family's two wagons and all their belongings crawled up an equally tall mountain and became stuck at the top?

It was a horrible question she wished she could ask someone. But who? She couldn't ask Pa. He was too busy. She couldn't ask Ma. That kind of question always gave her a fit of nerves. Eda couldn't ask Dick or Harry, the hired men, because they would surely make fun of her. As for her two sisters, she knew better than to ask them anything.

Eda kept her eyes straight ahead. Was this the way the Rocky Mountains would be from now on—all uphill? Her heart pounded in her ears and she could scarcely breathe. She held tight to the wagon and pretended to push. All the time she kept planning what she would do if the wagon started to tip over. If it went off the edge, she'd let go right away. Then she wouldn't be dragged into the valley with Lucy. Eda practiced opening and shutting her hands to make sure they'd come ungripped. She couldn't take any chances.

"What a view!" Belle said, almost laughing as she walked beside Eda in the thin, bright sunshine. Dust coated her curly brown hair. Dirt and sweat streaked her pretty face.

Eda refused to look at the view. She wanted to go back to flat, predictable Erie County, Pennsylvania, where there were no dizzy mountain passes to make her hands sweat.

Suddenly a rear wheel skittered out into thin air. The wagon groaned and pitched. Lucy screamed. Dirt and rocks cascaded downward and vanished over the cliff. *Pock-pockety-pock.* Pebbles and loose stones hurtled down from the wagons on the switchback above them. *Ping-pock-pock-ping.* Eda hunched her shoulders forward. Rocks bounced and ricocheted. She imagined wagons tumbling, twisting, and splintering as oxen writhed and lowed piteously. And beneath the wreckage she saw herself and her family squashed flat.

"Steady!" Pa commanded.

Harry, the bowlegged hired man who drove the first wagon, cracked the whip. The oxen plodded forward, pulling all four wheels back onto the trail. Red-haired Dick, the hired man in charge of the second wagon, threatened the oxen with colorful oaths. Miraculously the wagons kept moving.

Eda forced her legs to work again. She trudged up the endless incline. Hours seemed to drag by. Hot sun bored through the top of her floppy bonnet. Her throat was parched, and her teeth felt gritty with dust.

"How much farther?" Lucy whined from inside the wagon.

"Shut up, Lucy," Eda said in a low voice. "At least you don't have to walk."

Lucy thrust her head out of the back of the wagon. "What did you say?"

"Nothing."

Lucy turned and spoke to Ma as if Eda had suddenly become invisible. "I hope Eda is not making fun of my infirmity. That would be very un-Christian of her."

Ma sighed. She adjusted her crushed feathered hat. Her fashionable blue hoopskirt fluttered in the wind like a dirty kite. "Apologize," Ma rasped at Eda. Even though they were 12,000 feet above sea level and barely able to breathe, Ma seemed determined to keep up appearances and maintain her dignity. She was, after all, a Derleth—a member of the finest, oldest family in Erie County.

"Why do I have to say I'm sorry?" Eda squinted and pushed harder. Maybe with enough muscle, she'd shove Lucy right over the edge.

"Say it," Ma commanded. Her mouth moved, as if she was going to gasp something else, but no words came out. Still, Eda knew exactly what her mother wanted to say. She would tell Eda how poor martyred Lucy suffered her lameness like a true saint, how her sister had to be respected and protected from life's discomforts. Lucy was, after all, living proof of God's goodness, the most pious young woman in all of Erie County. Lucy was never allowed to leave the house or travel alone or visit anyone, for fear someone would comment on her unfortunate condition. Her lameness was a cross she would bear all her life.

"Mother! Make Eda say she's sorry!"

Sorry . . . sorry . . . sorry! Lucy's peevish whine echoed among the mountains.

"Must you always fight?" Pa shook his head. He stared at his wife and daughters as if they were strangers. Then he retreated to safety at the front of the first wagon.

"Sorry," Eda said in a squeezed-lemon voice. But deep down in her brat-baby heart, she wasn't sorry in the least.

Late that morning they finally arrived at the top of the pass. "Here we are!" Pa cried and waved his hat in the air. His shiny pink bald head gleamed in the sunlight.

The wagons stopped, and the exhausted oxen were unharnessed. Eda staggered a few feet away from the wagon and flopped down on the ground, breathless and glad to have solid, flat earth beneath her. When she opened her eyes, she saw miniature flowers that seemed to hug the mountaintop. Some were bright yellow with fat furry stems and quivering petals. Others were as sturdy as reeds. They shivered in the wind smelling of hot sun and something spicy, like sage and Christmas trees and dust.

Eda lifted her head and looked about. A clear, cold breeze cut right through her. She sat up, hugged her elbows against herself, and surveyed the strange treeless meadow flecked with rocks covered with orange lichens. To her amazement, she spied familiar white heaps. Snow—in summer!

Cautiously she stood up. More snow-topped mountains gnawed the horizon and rolled away one after the other in shades of gray and blue and black. She could see forever. She turned, marveling at the way the galloping clouds headed for distant valleys. It seemed like a strange, secret landscape that no one else had ever seen. Deep in the valleys, miles and miles and miles away, she could just make out spindly white gashes she knew must be roaring rivers.

Splat! Something stinging cold smacked Eda on the back of her neck. She screamed.

Belle shrieked with laughter. She packed another snowball and let it fly. Eda leaped to her feet and scooped up her own handful. She stuffed the crusty snow down her sister's dress, then ran away before Belle could catch her.

"Girls!" Ma called. "Don't go near the edge."

The edge! Eda stopped. She had forgotten about the edge. She shielded her face with her arms as her sister pummeled her with more snow. "Stop!" she cried. "I give up! You win!"

Belle pelted her hard with one last icy snowball.

"I said stop!" Eda said. She didn't want her sister to see her cry. It was foolish to cry now. She hadn't fallen over the edge. She was safe, wasn't she?

"All right, all right," Belle said in a gentle voice. She brushed the snow from Eda's hair as if she were a very young child. Then Belle sat down on a flat rock and patted a grassy place. "Sit here and rest," she said. "I won't throw any more snow. I promise."

Before she sat down, Eda quickly looked away

so her sister wouldn't see her wipe away her tears with her sleeve.

From her pocket, Belle produced a folded piece of paper. "I'd like to hear what you think about my first column for the *North East Gazette*. I want you to be completely honest—but please don't tell Ma. I'm getting paid one dollar, Mr. Mead said, for every hundred words I write. Ma wouldn't approve."

Eda rested her elbows on her knees and her chin in her palms. A dollar sounded like an incredibly large amount of money to her. "Does she think Mr. Mead should pay you more?"

Belle laughed. "Ladies don't write for newspapers. Ma says it's unseemly."

Eda sighed. Belle seemed to have all the luck. She was writing and getting paid. What more could anyone ask? "I won't tell Mother."

Belle glanced quickly over her shoulder and read aloud:

❧

July 14, 1864

Dearest Readers:
    We have traveled across the plains and are well on our way into the rugged

mountains to find riches in the Pikes
Peak region. We have taken a round-
about way, which I will take pains to
recount. We journeyed from our Pennsylvania home near the New York border by
train to Cleveland. Having heard that the
steamboats on the Great Lakes are quite
luxurious and used by the best people,
we boarded a boat named *Dean Richmond*.
This splendid craft, costing $100,000, was
280 feet long. Immediately, it ran into a
sand bar. Once we freed ourselves, our
conveyance took us safely up the Detroit
River, where we could see Canada.

Our voyage took us through Lake St.
Clair and River St. Clair and arrived in
Lake Huron. Heavy fog forced us to don
life jackets. We did not make good time
as we had to stop constantly for wood.
Finally, we passed through the Straits at
Mackinac and made the long uneventful
journey south to Milwaukee. The cost of
this lake trip was nearly $400, but worth
every penny for a group of travelers who

have no servants yet wish to be surrounded by the finer things of life. I can not recommend Chicago—a filthy swamp town. Gratefully, we left Chicago and made our way by train posthaste to the tiny burg of Quincy, Illinois. We crossed the Mississippi River on a boat named the *Rosa Tyler*. On the opposite shore we again found ourselves traveling by noisy train to St. Joseph, Missouri. Here our covered wagon adventure began.

We saw no buffalo as they have been driven south by Indians. We passed Kearney City and on through Julesburg on a road filled with emigrants—all bound for the same place and the same object: gold. We spied quite a number of Indians on the Great American Desert. They appeared friendly but they are an ignorant miserable race of beings. Once in Colorado, however, the Indians became more brutish. We camped at one spot where a family was massacred only two weeks ago. I did not relish my dinner much on account of fear, but we were not molested.

Once we reached Denver, the great metropolis of the West, the sight of some decent buildings seemed very cheering after our long journey through a barren, empty land. Some buildings were made of sod; others are made of brick. There are ten thousand people in Denver from different parts of the world—from the well dressed lady to the barefoot beggar. My sister and myself were invited by a young gentleman of my father's acquaintance to attend a concert in Denver given by the Colorado band (as this gentleman read the advertisement). We looked in at the window before entering and found it was a *colored* band. Since we did not wish to be seen in such an establishment, we walked around the city instead.

This morning we commence our first experience climbing mountains—an adventure which I will save for my next installment . . .

> Faithfully submitted by
> Correspondent S.B.H.
> Colorado Territory

"Not bad," Eda said.

"Not bad? That's all you have to say?"

"You forgot to tell about the rattlesnake under the wagon," Eda said, trying to be as completely honest as she could. "And what about the time we threw a bucket of water down a hole to capture a prairie dog? Remember how the prairie dog walked away, dripping wet and glaring at us? I bet he never had such treatment from girls before."

"That was childish," Belle said coldly. "I'm writing for grown-ups, you know."

Eda flashed her sister a conciliatory smile. She didn't want to upset Belle, especially when for once she was treating her like a real person. "The part about the Indian massacre was very vivid. Your readers will certainly enjoy that."

Belle folded her paper and tucked it back inside her pocket. "You think so?"

"Absolutely. All the papers are full of Indian massacre stories. But"—Eda paused cautiously—"why don't you use your name at the end? Why don't you write 'Sarah Belle Hitchcock' instead of 'S.B.H.'?"

"Because," Belle said, leaning back on her elbows, "lady writers sign just their initials. And of

course I don't want Ma to know about my splendid new career."

"Of course," Eda mumbled. She was sure that
if she had a splendid new career like Belle's, she'd
sign her whole name in big letters, just for the
thrill of seeing it in print. She wouldn't care what
Ma said.

Eda and Belle sat together in companionable
silence watching from a distance as Lucy
climbed clumsily out of the wagon. Pa helped
her down to the ground. When Lucy stood up,
she was almost as tall as Pa. He was a small
man with broad shoulders. He had fine laughing blue eyes and a ruddy beard, which he
kept trimmed and neat. "Pa would look very
handsome in a soldier's uniform, don't you
think?" Belle asked.

Eda nodded. But deep down she didn't care
what anybody whispered back home. She was
glad that Pa had not gone away to fight.

"From here Lucy looks like anybody else,"
Belle said. She plucked and twirled a little yellow
flower, gazing at it the same way she admired
her lovely reflection in a mirror.

Eda had to agree with Belle. From a distance,
Lucy appeared almost pretty. Her thick auburn

hair somehow looked lustrous against her somber gray dress. It was only when Lucy gripped her walking stick and took a few steps that she revealed her handicap. Lucy rocked in an exaggerated way when she walked. Since birth one of her legs had been shorter than the other. One foot was so badly deformed she had to wear a special shoe.

Eda could not see Lucy's expression, but she knew that her pale face was tense and concentrated. She could imagine how Lucy's mouth looked, screwed tight and hard and determined, and how she shifted her brown eyes every which way, hoping desperately that no stranger was watching.

"Eda, you must be kinder to our eldest sister," Belle announced, sounding suspiciously like Ma.

Eda frowned. "I think everyone is kind enough to Lucy. I think Lucy should be kinder to *us.*"

"She can't."

"Why not?"

"Something's wrong with her heart."

Eda looked at her sister quizzically. What was she talking about? It was Lucy's leg not her heart that was damaged. Eda was silent for several moments, desperately trying to think of something interesting to say so that her sister wouldn't become bored and walk away. To Eda, Belle seemed like a creature from a more fortunate sphere. Belle had her own interests, her own pleasures. She seemed so grown up and self-assured that sitting beside her made Eda feel small and insignificant. Now that Belle had shared her newspaper column, Eda wanted to share one of her two deepest, darkest secrets. "Someday," she said and took a deep breath, "I'm going away to college."

"College? Whatever for, little one?" Belle said, smiling unpleasantly. She reached over and twirled the yellow flower under Eda's chin.

Eda pushed Belle's hand away. She jumped to her feet and gave her skirt a fierce shake. When would her sisters stop treating her like a baby? She stomped away.

"Where do you think you're going?" Belle called after her.

"As far away as I can," Eda replied and kept walking. She was on an important errand. She needed to be alone so that she could write something right away in her journal before she forgot:

Thoughts by the way. And why not! Others think and why not I! Artists are wrong. When you look at the top of a mountain from a distance, it seems like a sharp point but when you arrive, you discover there's a good deal of land. A perfect place to strand all the older sisters in the world.

Chapter 2

The long hard descent into the valley late that afternoon was more terrifying than the climb up. Pa and the two hired men had to lodge a long log between the back wheels of each wagon to slow the descent. The wagons slid down the steep slope, wheels locked. Eda trudged behind the wagons. Her knees wobbled and her legs ached by the time they finally arrived on level ground again.

After several more days of traveling and camping in abandoned cabins, the Hitchcock family and their two hired men came to what was called Middle Park. This broad green valley cradled between the mountains extended three hundred miles in length and five to fifty miles in width. The rolling, open grassland and friendly groves of trees along the streams reminded Eda of home.

Memories of Pennsylvania made her think of Dragonbreath, her best friend back home. His real name was Wallace Edward Dillard, and he had the most rotten teeth and foul breath of any thirteen-year-old boy at school. She never called him Wallace. No one did. Everyone called him Dragonbreath. He didn't mind. Names like Wallace Edward, he said, were cruel inventions passed along by parents who wished to torment their children. Dragonbreath better fit the image he had of himself—stalwart, brave, indomitable. Of course, Eda did not think he was any of these things. Her friend was bookish, slope-shouldered, and awkward. But she missed him all the same.

Dragonbreath was the only person to whom she had ever revealed her second deepest, darkest secret: that she planned one day to write an original epic tragedy and have it performed in some exciting place, like London. Her play would be miles and miles better than *The Ragpicker of Paris*, which she'd seen at the opera house back home. When the curtain fell and the audience stopped sobbing in the London theater, she imagined how the people would jump to their feet and shout "Bravo! Bravo!" They'd call her the new Shakespeare. And of course she'd have to go on stage and bow and blush and bow some more and say, "Oh, really, thank you so very much!" Dragonbreath would be in the audience, too, only all grown up. He'd whistle very loud, and people would stomp their feet and—

"Harriet Adelle Hitchcock, do you hear me?" Ma demanded. "I have been trying to speak to you for the past five minutes, yet you just stare into space as if you've lost your senses."

"Sorry, ma'am," Eda said.

"We will stop here so that you may wash and comb your hair and put on your best clean dress."

"Why?" Eda asked.

"We're coming to a town," Ma said.

Dick chuckled. "Fairplay's not much of a town from what I hear."

"All the same, you never know who we might meet," Ma insisted. "It's always best to make a good first impression."

While the oxen grazed and rested, Belle spent more than an hour trying to decide which of her many dresses to wear. She rearranged her hair three times, finally choosing what she called a simple rustic look.

Meanwhile, Eda gazed at her own reflection in a pool of still water. No amount of primping and brushing would improve her appearance, she decided. Her ears were too big. Her face was too freckled. Her mouth was too wide. She parted her hair in the middle and tied around her head her only clean ribbon. She rubbed her front teeth with a corner of her apron and lightly splashed some water on her cheeks. Her finest feature was her dark, penetrating eyes. If only she had fluttery, thick eyelashes like Belle! As it was, she decided her looks were nothing more than ordinary.

Ma bustled about, coaxing the girls into the wagon again. It was plain that she held little hope for Lucy's attractions. "Come along, dear," Ma said impatiently as Lucy made one more quick adjustment of her hair, which was trapped in a severe black net at the nape of her neck. "No need to fuss."

Lucy looked disappointed but did as she was told.

As they approached Fairplay, ditches and

heaps of stone and gravel pocked the landscape. Stumps dotted the hillsides. Streams flowed brown and turbid. "Looks like some good gulch mining here," Pa said approvingly.

While her sisters were busy looking at the bleak scenery, Eda took out her journal and, in her special code, wrote:

We are soon to enter the city of Fairplay where we expect to meet some of the Rocky Mountain aristocracy. This is the first city we have seen since leaving Denver.

"What are you writing?"

Belle's amused voice made Eda jump. "Nothing," Eda said and slammed the little book shut.

"Strange writing you've got there. Didn't they teach you how to spell at school?" Belle demanded. "Almost looks like another language. If you'd like, I could—"

"No, thanks," Eda interrupted. She smiled mysteriously and did not say another word. She was glad her sister could not read what she'd written. She'd have to be more careful. What if Belle found her journal and decoded her entries?

The wagon bumped and lurched into town—a homely place with nothing more than six or eight crude pine log cabins about six feet high with poles laid on for roofs covered with dirt. Each had a single door and window. On the top of one building were large deer antlers.

"There's the hotel," Harry said, pointing. "And there's the saloon. They call it a deadfall in these parts."

"Deadfall," Eda repeated the marvelous word to help remember to write it in her journal.

A girl with dramatic red curls and a startling pink dress stood gazing at Eda and her sisters from the saloon doorway as if she'd seldom seen another girl in all her days. Her face was very pale. Her lips were very red. Eda waved, delighted to see anyone in this forlorn, deserted place.

"Don't," Ma commanded. "Keep your eyes forward and don't even look at her."

Lucy and Belle did exactly as Ma demanded. They sat up straight and tall as if the girl in the doorway were invisible.

"Why can't we say hello? You said you wanted to go visiting," Eda demanded. "She seems friendly enough." She knew that Ma had a strange way of snubbing certain women at home. Sometimes she snubbed women who lived in houses she said were too fancy. Sometimes she snubbed women who lived in houses she said were too plain. There was no predicting who Ma would snub.

"Really, Eda, can't you see?" Lucy said. "That creature is fallen. Utterly depraved. A woman of easy virtue."

"Don't you know anything?" Belle hissed.

Eda felt her face flush. She disliked being thought of as a blundering little girl, a mere stupid child. "What is easy virtue?" she demanded.

Ma looked horrified. "You're too young to understand," she said. "It's not nice to ask about such things."

Eda twisted around to study the fascinating girl one last time. She'd never seen anyone utterly depraved before. How could Ma and her sisters be sure? Maybe it was the girl's hairstyle and face paint. Back home, women wore their long hair swept back in what they called a waterfall, secured with a net behind the neck. The pale girl in the doorway had a mass of short Titian-red curls clustered atop her head and falling over her eyebrows, which were darkly arched as if drawn with a pencil. Her mouth was the color of over-ripe plums. Each cheek was daubed brilliant red.

"If women, prompted by no other motive than to please men, paint their faces, they are going a false route and will only render themselves horrible," Lucy announced in her most pious voice. She looked directly at Belle, whose face flushed.

"She didn't look horrible," Eda mumbled. "She was rather attractive. I wish I had such striking hair."

"Really, Eda!" Lucy clucked in outrage.

Belle stifled a giggle.

Ma dabbed her temples with her rose water–scented handkerchief. "Harriet Adelle Hitchcock," Ma murmured, "you shock me."

Eda hunched forward, wishing she could disappear. She was ridiculed and considered stupid for not knowing what she had been expressly forbidden to ask about. It wasn't fair.

Finally, Pa halted the wagon and climbed out to help Ma to the ground. A pair of abandoned burros with their ribs showing wandered past. Ma looked up and down Fairplay's main thoroughfare with disappointment. "This is not what I expected, Mr. Hitchcock," she told Pa.

Pa shrugged and motioned to Dick and Harry. "We're going to see about finding good claims. You can wander about and do some shopping while we're gone."

"Shopping?" Ma sputtered. "Where can one shop in a place like this?"

Pa did not make any suggestions. He hurried off toward the saloon.

"Where should we go first?" Eda said eagerly.

"I'm not going anywhere," Lucy replied. "I'm staying right here in the wagon. This town is barbaric."

"I like it," Eda said. "Come on, Belle. Come with me. We'll go to the dry goods store. Maybe they've got a post office. There might be a letter for us. Or perhaps you can mail a letter." She winked, hoping her sister would appreciate her interest in promoting her splendid new career.

Belle brightened considerably. She leaped from the wagon.

"What about Lucy?" Ma demanded. She opened her green silk parasol with a loud thump to scare away a mangy stray dog. "It is unseemly to have her waiting here alone."

"Belle and I will only be gone a short time," Eda promised. She didn't want to be trapped in the wagon with Lucy. Lucy who would make her read Scripture and then scold her for her mistakes. "We might not have a chance to go into a store again for weeks."

"You are selfish, unfeeling girls," Ma announced. She climbed back into the wagon. "I'll stay with your poor sister."

Gleefully, Eda grabbed Belle's arm and hurried across the street. She did not feel the least bit guilty about abandoning Lucy.

"We'll be right back," Belle called gaily to their mother and sister as she skipped around a pile of horse manure.

Eda and Belle entered the small, dark store that said "Dry Goods" on a peeling hand-painted sign over the doorway. Nothing seemed the way she remembered back in Pennsylvania. Pa's store had been cluttered with crowded shelves of tobacco jars, kitchen wares, bolts of cloth, crockery, and canned goods. Barrels had stood in the aisles filled with flour and molasses and crackers. Displayed in shining glass cases were hats and school slates and fishhooks and hair tonic. Pa's store had smelled of cheese, coffee, leather, vinegar, peppermint, and kerosene.

The store in Fairplay was remarkably empty. There was little for sale besides mealy flour, miners' tin pans and picks, and a few jugs of whiskey. A big scale stood on the counter. The store smelled of wet dog and stale whiskey. The tall, thin storekeeper looked up at them from his copy of the *Rocky Mountain News*. "I got some string beans here hauled one hundred miles. Sell them to you for twenty-five cents a pound." He gestured toward a basket of green beans nearly as wizened and dried up as his own face.

"Sir, we're not interested in green beans," Belle said. "We're wondering if you might have any letters for us."

"Name?"

"Hitchcock, sir," Belle said.

The storekeeper rummaged through a box of stained, curled papers. "We got a few letters come in since the last Indian menace. They attacked a stagecoach outside of Cherry Creek, killed the driver and dumped most of the mail in a ditch." He shook his head. "Not much new here. If it ain't Indians burning ranches it's Confederate sympathizers attacking pack trains. Some people call them guerrillas. They've been robbing and murdering travelers up and down the pass. Where you greenhorns headed?"

Eda shivered. Indians burning ranches? Guerrillas attacking travelers? She assumed the only treacherous Indians were on the plains and the only treacherous Rebels were fighting back in the

States. Why hadn't Pa mentioned that these dangers also existed in the mountains?

"Our father is going to prospect," Belle announced. "He's at the saloon right now seeking directions." She craned her neck, trying to peer into the basket of mail.

"Gold dust is currency here," the storekeeper said. "Takes a pinch of twenty-five cents' worth to pay postage for a letter. Next postal rider for Denver comes through here next week. You got any gold dust?"

Belle frowned, insulted. "We just arrived, so we have not yet had time to strike it rich. But I do have money and a letter to send." She reached inside her pocket and produced a folded envelope addressed to Mr. Mead at the *North East Gazette* in Erie County, Pennsylvania. From her coin purse she fished out a shining silver dollar. "Will this do?"

The storekeeper turned over the shining coin suspiciously. "Don't see many of these from the States," he grumbled.

"A dollar is far more than I owe you," she said, then softened her expression into a smile that would have melted butter. "You sure you don't have something for us?"

The storekeeper reached inside his pocket and

pulled out a battered envelope. "This says Hitch-cock, I believe."

Belle licked her lips and handed him the coin. "You may keep the change."

Eagerly, Belle and Eda took the letter outdoors into the bright sunlight. "It's been opened!" Eda said with dismay. "I'll bet he read every word. Doesn't he know a person's mail is private?"

"He's got nothing else to do all day. Here, give it to me," Belle said. "I think it's from Auntie."

"Shouldn't we wait and show Ma first?" Eda asked.

But Belle had already slipped the letter from the envelope and was reading aloud:

❧

June 11, 1864

Dearest Sister, Amory, Belle, Lucy and Harriet:

I hope this epistle finds you all well and on your way to new riches as your credi-tors are looking for you and I am spending most of my days telling these rude gentle-men that you have left town and I do not

know whether you will ever be back to
Pennsylvania again.

❧

"What's a creditor?" Eda asked in a small,
stubborn voice.

Belle rolled her eyes. "A creditor is someone
Pa owes money to."

"And what does she mean when she says we
might never return?"

Belle sniffed. "You are very ignorant for someone who thinks she might one day go to college."

Eda bit her lip and felt more worried than ever.

"Now stop interrupting and let me finish,"
Belle said and continued reading aloud:

❧

The weather here has been abominably hot
and muggy for so early in the summer and
my garden wilts. We have had regular
meetings of the sanitary commission and
knitted more than one hundred pairs of
socks to send to the Brave soldiers. I am
my self baking a dozen pies and donating
several of my best plum jams for the raffle
to raise money for medicines. School held

an Onion Day to collect produce for soldiers as well, but we are of course weary when we hear how badly the war drags on. Mrs. Norton's boy died of dysentery and he never fired a shot. We hear there's typhoid in the camps and I hope James will return unharmed God willing. Of course none of this affects you so far from all our Troubles. We pray the Indians will let you pass safe and that all your girls will be spared. We hear stories that Indians take no prisoners. We hear about scalpings and hideous tortures. Such brutality toward captives! I know Lucy and Belle will keep the Sabbath but I imagine Harriet as hoopless and shoeless standing with arms akimbo, mouth extended, tongue protruding, nose contracted, surveying the wonders of this wonderfully wonderful world. I hope my dear niece has not already changed so much I can not recognize her. As for you, dear Sister, I hope that I will see you again in this Life time. I enclose a lock of my hair as remembrance.

Your loving sister,
Mathilda

❧

Eda clenched her fists. "Arms akimbo! Tongue protruding! What does she take me for? Some kind of squaw?"

Belle laughed. "She's only joking. You know Auntie Till."

"When we go home, she'll see that she's wrong. I haven't changed at all."

"You'll wait a long time for that, Eda. I doubt we'll ever go back to Pennsylvania."

Eda took a deep breath. "That's a cruel thing to say. I don't believe you." She thought of Dragonbreath and could not bear the idea of never seeing him again.

"Have you been asleep all these months," Belle asked in a superior voice, "or have you just refused to notice what's been happening?" She tucked the letter back in her pocket and strode off.

For several moments, Eda was too stunned to speak. What was Belle talking about? Nobody had said the move to Colorado might be forever. She always thought they'd go home after Pa struck it rich.

Eda walked a few steps. *"Have you been asleep all these months?"*—Belle's words rang in her ears. Desperately, Eda tried to remember what had happened before they left Pennsylvania. She recalled angry late-night conversations between her parents. Nothing new about that. She also remembered her mother's fits. Nothing new about those, either. Ma was always having attacks of the nerves. But what about those men from the bank with the stovepipe hats and sober expressions like ministers at funerals? Then there was the closing of Pa's store. And afterward the way the other students looked differently at her at school. Eda had thought they were only envious of her because she was going west on a great adventure.

What else? What else? Eda tried to think. The house was sold and many of their belongings were carted away. Wasn't that necessary to make room for what they needed to take on their long trip? "We'll strike it rich in no time," Pa had kept telling them. Always cheerful. Always optimistic.

And of course Eda had believed him.

Now she wondered, what if he'd lied? What if

they had all lied to her? Ma and her sisters, too. Perhaps they'd never told her what was really happening because they assumed she was too young to understand. Looking back, she saw that even Auntie Till hadn't been honest. Before Eda left, Auntie had given her such insulting, babyish advice. "Eda dear, remember on your journey not to swallow a live buffalo," she had said as if she thought it was terribly funny.

Eda's brow furrowed as she trudged toward the wagon. Nobody ever told her the truth. Nobody took her seriously.

"Oh, my word! What a wonderful surprise," Ma exclaimed. She sat inside the wagon, admiring the lock of gray hair and reading Aunt Mathilda's letter aloud over and over again. Eda refused to listen. Only her sisters seemed enthralled.

Eventually, Pa returned, full of news about a claim in a place twelve miles away called Young America Gulch. "And look here, girls. See what I bought special for you?" he said proudly.

Harry led a gentle, cream-colored Indian pony to the wagon.

"Whatever made you decide to purchase such

a creature, Mr. Hitchcock?" Ma demanded. "Our funds are limited, I'll have you remember."

Creditors. Eda recoiled a little thinking of the ominous-sounding word again.

"This pony was a great bargain," Pa said. "The owners were practically giving the creature away. He'll be a great help to Lucy."

"Lucy!" Ma sputtered. "She is not a horseback rider."

"Well then, I'll ride him," Belle announced. She patted the horse's sturdy brown neck. The pony immediately searched her pocket for a treat. She broke off a piece of hard biscuit, which he ate eagerly.

"What's the matter, Eda? Don't you like the pony?" Pa asked.

"I like it fine," Eda said stiffly. "Only I'd like to know something: are we ever going back to Pennsylvania?"

Pa and Ma seemed to be taken aback by this question. Belle and Lucy frowned at Eda as if she was spoiling everything. Pa scratched his head. Then he grinned, the way he did when he was about to tell a favorite joke. "It is my fervent hope never to go back unless I am a very wealthy man," he said.

Harry clapped a hand on Dick's shoulder and shouted, "Hear! Hear!"

"We'll all soon be rich men!" Harry replied. He hooked his thumbs in his invisible fancy lapels, stuck out his skinny elbows and strutted like a proud gold tycoon. Everyone laughed.

Everyone except Eda.

Chapter 3

After traveling up hill and down, we came to the valley of the Arkansaw. This is a beautiful river running in a south easterly direction. Its current is very rapid the water is deep. Our gulch is called Young America. It is two miles in length, and our cabin stands near the foot of it so near the Arkansaw that the roarings of its waters can be plainly heard. It is very lovely here but quite retired there being no family near us. Wild creatures and savages abound.

As Dick and Harry began unloading the Hitchcock family's many possessions into the deserted cabin, Harry sang:

"If I was at home and alive again,
I'd have a different life.
I'd have my fill of pie and cake
And stay with my dear little wife."

Ma stood in the middle of the moldering cabin, her fists on her stout hips. Her dark eyes narrowed as she surveyed the hard-packed dirt floor and the scattered, rotting packing cases left behind by the former owner. A stained wagon sheet had been stretched across the ceiling to keep dirt from drifting down from the sod-covered roof. The only light in the windowless cabin came through the doorway and around the stovepipe where the hole in the ceiling had been cut too large. There was no real door, only a filthy saddle blanket hung in the doorway with rocks tied in two corners to keep the blanket from blowing open. "We cannot stay here, Mr. Hitchcock," Ma announced. "This place is unspeakable."

"We won't live in this house forever, Emily," Pa murmured. "It's not bad, compared to the other places we stayed on our way here. At least this cabin has a roof."

"A roof? Is *that* all that matters to you?" Ma

lowered herself on to a packing case and buried her soft pink face in a lace handkerchief. "First you take away my servants. Then you drag me and my three refined daughters out here, where we are in constant danger of being attacked by savages. Now you force us to live in this hovel. I don't think I can bear much more."

Pa cleared his throat. "Eda, Belle, Lucy, will you go outside for a little while so that I might speak to your mother in private?"

Obediently, Belle and Lucy hurried out of the cabin to prepare supper, but Eda lingered in the yard and pretended to dust the unpacked melodeon. She was determined to stay within earshot so that she could hear every word her parents were saying. If no one would tell her what was going on, she would secretly search for the truth any way she could.

"Emily," Pa said in a voice that carried easily through the blackened, unchinked log walls. "You're too tightly wound. Everything will be fine. This place is only temporary. Once I strike it rich, we'll have enough money to live anywhere you want."

"Anywhere?" Ma said. She sniffed loudly.

"San Francisco, New York—anywhere you like."

San Francisco? New York? Eda sidled closer, waiting for him to mention Erie County. Just as she pressed her ear to the wall, however, Harry came around the corner with a bucket. "You can take this and fetch some water from the river down a ways. That would be a sight more help than eavesdropping," Harry said, winking.

Eda blushed. She took the bucket. "Is Lucy cooking?"

Harry nodded and puckered his whiskered face into a grin. "She ain't poisoned us yet."

Eda groaned. "It's not as if she hasn't tried." She heaved the bucket over her arm and set off at a gallop. *"It is my fervent hope never to go back unless I am a very wealthy man,"* Pa had said. Well, if they were lucky, he might have a strike before the end of the summer. Then perhaps they'd be on their way home again. What was so hard about prospecting? Dick had told her about one Colorado man who had such an excellent claim and found so much gold that he was forced to store his riches in anything handy he could find— pots, pans, even a pair of old boots!

Maybe Eda could help Pa. Maybe she could

start looking right now. She searched the ground and saw a handsome rock. She gave it a nudge with her toe. She picked up the rock, spit on it, and shined it with the hem of her dress. It was sparkly and reddish. Harry would know if it was real gold. She put it in her pocket.

Eda followed the sound of gurgling, splashing, and rumbling. As she walked, the woods became darker, then darker still. Suddenly she stopped. She cocked her head to one side. What was that? Somewhere in the piney underbrush she had heard a noisy scratch and scuffle, then silence.

"Eda!" Lucy's high-pitched call resounded through the woods. "Water!"

Eda took a few steps toward the river and dipped the bucket into the cold current. Something bright red flashed and vanished among the trees on the other side.

A pair of eyes.

She yanked the heavy bucket out of the water and rushed all the way back to the cabin, her head filled with visions of flying tomahawks and masked guerrillas. "Here," she said, her hands shaking uncontrollably.

Lucy leaned over the smoky fire stirring something black and foul-smelling in a kettle. "That's hardly enough water for my purposes."

"Tell Belle to get more," Eda said. "I don't know why I always have to get water. She never does anything."

"Don't complain to me. I should be taking a rest cure, not slaving over a hot fire." Lucy smacked a piece of sticky biscuit dough between her hands. The rubbery white stuff webbed between her fingers. She looked as if she might cry at any moment as she tried to shake it loose.

Eda wiped her dirty hands on the back of her dress. She tugged dough from her sister's fingers. Only with great effort was Eda able to pinch off small, bullet-size lumps, which she dropped into a pan. "Now what do I do?" She stared at the gray, gritty dough balls.

"You have to cook them, of course," Lucy said angrily.

Eda sighed. It was so difficult being kind to Lucy. No matter how hard Eda tried, Lucy only became nastier. Eda set the pan atop the hot coals and watched the small biscuits shrivel up.

Belle beat the side of an empty kettle with a wooden spoon. "Dinner!"

People helped themselves to the food and stood

around the smoky fire with their tin plates. "These biscuits are burned on the outside and raw on the inside," Belle said with disgust.

"Eda cooked them. Blame her," Lucy said. She dumped her own food on the ground and stomped into the wagon.

Pa made a low whistling sound. "Well, there's always canned peaches and crackers and coffee."

"Please don't think ill of Lucy," Ma said. "It's a trial for her to cook, you know. I'd help her if I knew how. But my nerves . . . my nerves . . ."

Eda glanced angrily at her sister's spilled food. If she or Belle had done that, they'd be scolded severely. But Lucy could be as rude as she wished and no one said anything. It wasn't fair.

Pa nudged his burned salt pork into a neat pile on his plate. "I'll have some more of those canned peaches. They're real tasty. Why, when I ran the store —"

"Please, let's not bring up that subject," Ma interrupted. "My nerves have been wrecked enough already."

Harry and Dick gave each other amused

glances and quickly finished their coffee. No one spoke for several moments.

Belle cleared her throat politely. "I was quite touched today by the little graves we saw along the roadside. Every now and again I came across one of these with a little picket fence around it and a deserted and forlorn house nearby, and I just began to wonder."

Eda suddenly didn't feel one bit hungry. She glanced at the cabin. "What do you think happened to the . . . the people?"

"They come out, settle down," Harry said between swallows of coffee. "They're either prospecting or sawing up timber. When they fail to find any ore or they cut down all the trees, they move off somewheres else."

"These houses are just rough log huts," Pa growled. "Can't say they're a considerable loss."

"No," Belle said slowly, "but they were once someone's home."

"Indians run off a lot of people," Dick said. "Can't trust Indians. Especially those Utes. A despicable, treacherous race."

"Do Utes have red eyes?" Eda asked in a quiet voice.

"Red eyes?" Dick said and spit. "Mountain

lions got red eyes. Utes don't have no color at all in the dark. That's what makes them invisible at night."

Eda felt sweat trickle down the inside of her arms.

Harry snickered. "Don't pay him no mind, gal. He likes to spook folks."

Dick smiled bashfully, but Eda did not feel reassured. That night Pa kept the fire going in the little stove. Eda wrapped a quilt around her shoulders. She took out her journal and wrote:

Writing in my Dear Little Journal is more restful than a conversation. This is my only companion, the one place I can go where I will not be ridiculed for what I am not allowed to understand. Before we left Pennsylvania my older cousin Grace told me that babies are not found in flowers but in people. I felt a vague sense of contamination hearing this and so tonight I had enough courage to ask Ma. She gave me a severe scolding, which has left me with a penetrating sense of Not-niceness. I have decided this will keep me from pursuing my investigation any further. Perhaps married people have children because God sees the minister marrying them through the church roof.

Eda paused to make sure Ma wasn't awake. She glanced at her sleeping sisters.

Belle would be disgraced if she knew how disgusting she looks when she snores. Her mouth hangs open and there's spittle coming out of one corner. All her beaus back in Pennsylvania would be shocked. As for Lucy, she sneers even when she sleeps. I wonder how I look when I sleep. I'm sure I don't drool.

Eda tucked her journal under her pillow. When she shut her eyes, she saw ghosts of the people who had lived in the cabin—the ones who had never found gold. The ones who couldn't even make a living chopping down trees.

Something deep in the woods screeched hungrily. Wolves howled. Eda's eyes flew open. In the darkness she imagined silent, stealthy Indians padding around the cabin and peering through the cracks in the walls. She tried to keep her eyes open, but she was so terribly tired. Little by little she drifted off to sleep.

In the middle of the night, a heavy body brushed against the outside wall of the cabin—*whoosh.* Eda awoke suddenly. She thought of the door covered only with a saddle blanket. "Somebody's out there," she whispered. She wished she had a real weapon, not just a rock in her pocket.

Belle sat up. "Who is it?"

Whoosh—bristling around the corner.

"I don't know." Eda's hand trembled. She reached for the rock. She held it tight, ready to throw.

"Maybe it's Dick or Harry," Belle whispered hopefully. "They're sleeping outside near the wagon."

Whoosh—shaking dirt from the roof. "Sounds too big," Eda said. "Wake up Pa."

Pa was already awake. He fumbled for his gun and rushed outside. Eda pulled the blanket up over her head and waited, scarcely breathing.

A shot rang out.

"Mr. Hitchcock!" Ma shouted.

"Pa's dead. I know he's dead," Lucy murmured and sniffed.

Eda threw off her blanket and grabbed a frying pan.

"What are you doing? You come back here," Ma ordered.

"Someone has to help Pa," Eda said.

Before she reached the door she heard familiar voices outside. Dick and Harry, sleepy and confused, were arguing. Pa stumbled back inside. "It's gone."

"Are you sure, Mr. Hitchcock?" Ma demanded.

"Everyone go back to sleep," Pa said. "I'll stay up and keep watch."

"Was it an Indian, Pa?" Eda demanded. "Was it a guerrilla?"

"I can't say. But whatever it was, it won't be back," Pa said, his voice weary. "Don't worry."

Eda lay down again. She closed her eyes and longed for morning.

When first light finally came dimly over the rims of the mountains, Eda woke. She wondered if the intruder had only been a bad dream. Bravely she tiptoed outside. What she saw took her breath away. "Come quick!" she shouted to Dick, who crouched nearby mending a harness.

Dick hurried closer. "What's the matter?"

Eda pointed at the unmistakable shape of a bare human footprint in the soft, damp ground. "Indians?"

"Bear," he said. "Old Bruin's footprint looks so much like a human's that the Indians say bears are an ancient tribe of people who wandered off on their own. Some claim that bears shift back and forth from human to bear to human again."

"Oh." Eda felt something twist in the bottom of her stomach. *Red eyes*. Maybe what she'd seen was Old Bruin.

"Bears scare off easy. Just make a loud noise," Dick said. "Don't bother them and they won't bother you."

Eda thought of something worse. "What if Indians or guerrillas come while you and Pa and Harry are gone prospecting?"

Dick scratched his head. "Your pa's leaving a gun."

Eda dug her toe into the soft dirt. She could just imagine Ma's hysterics if she or one of her sisters even touched the gun. "You know," she admitted, "we don't know how to shoot."

Dick smiled. "Nothing to it. Just point the gun and pull the trigger. Don't look so glum. We're not going far away. You see that hill?"

Eda nodded. It looked more like a mountain than a hill.

"If you climb to the top lickety-split and give a shout, we'll come running," Dick promised. "You're a resourceful gal. You'll be fine."

Eda stared at the steep, pine-covered slope and wondered how long it would take her to climb to the top.

Late that morning, Eda and her sisters watched sadly as Pa, Dick, and Harry shouldered their supplies and set off for the diggings farther down the gulch. "Don't worry, now," Pa told the girls. "We'll be back before you know it."

Ma was so distraught that she refused to leave the cabin to say good-bye. No matter how hard Ma tried, she could not convince Pa that it was his duty to stay and protect them.

"I can't prospect for gold if I'm holed up here," he told her. "Someone may jump our claim if we don't get moving."

When Eda spied the last glimpse of Pa through the trees, she and Belle came inside to make sure the gun was hanging on its pegs inside the doorway. Lucy sat in a corner. Ma perched at the melodeon, her well-kept hands resting on the ivory keys. Her eyes seemed to be staring at something far away.

"Are you going to play?" Eda asked hopefully.

Ma sighed. "If I'd had the opportunities you girls have, I would have been a very happy child. I always had musical talent, even though the only training I had consisted of foolish little songs and silly waltzes, and I had time for only fifteen minutes of practice a day."

"I might believe that I had unusual talent if I did not know what good music sounded like," Lucy replied in a bitter voice. "I might enjoy fifteen minutes' practice if I were busy and happy the rest of the day."

Belle glowered at her mother and her older sister. "What are you talking about? You don't know how useless life seems when all difficulties are removed. I have been simply smothered with advantages. I am sick of them. It is like eating a sweet cake first thing in the morning."

Ma did not look up from the melodeon. Lucy wrapped the coverlet around her tightly. Belle sat down at the table and ferociously paged through a well-thumbed copy of *Frank Leslie's Illustrated Newspaper.* All three were so deep in their private misery that none of them noticed Eda leave the cabin.

Pa was hardly out of sight and already they were fighting and complaining. How would Eda survive being trapped here with her cantankerous mother and sisters, never knowing when Pa would return? In disgust, Eda marched to the noisy river. She pulled the rock from her pocket and threw it as hard as she could into the water.

Smack! The river's singing current was so loud she could barely hear the splash.

Another awful thought raced into her head. Would Dick and Harry and Pa be able to hear her voice if she climbed the hill and called for help? Eda frowned. Maybe Dick had lied so that she would stop badgering him. Once again she suspected that she had been betrayed by grown-ups.

Chapter 4

The night after Pa and the hired men left, Eda and her sisters and their mother were too afraid to sleep. They felt certain that Indians, guerrillas, or bears would attack them in the dark. Eda spent the night clutching a jar of blinding hot cayenne pepper to hurl into the faces of stealthy Indians. Belle kept a pan of boiling water ready to throw at any unsuspecting guerrilla. Lucy sat with an ax in her lap, determined to protect herself from marauding bears. By the time morning came, everyone was cranky and exhausted. There had been no unusual noises, no intruders.

For the next seven nights, the girls tried to sit

up, listening. Each evening, however, their resolve began to wane until finally they were simply unable to keep their vigil. The moment they sat down, they fell asleep. Only Ma remained awake. In the morning, she yawned and warned her daughters, "Do not leave sight of the cabin. We can never be too careful." Then she flopped down on the bed and immediately began to snore.

Eda and her sisters crept out of the cabin into the sunshine. There were no tracks behind the cabin. No tracks anywhere. Eda felt restless. Her stomach growled. Since their arrival, she and her sisters and mother had had nothing to eat except crackers and marmalade, a tin of sardines, and a few cans of creamed corn. She decided she needed something more substantial or she would soon expire. "I've seen plenty of slow-moving fish in deep pools at the river's edge," Eda told her sisters. "All we have to do is wade into the water and scoop up a fish. How difficult can that be?"

"I don't know," Belle said anxiously. "What if Ma wakes up and finds out we've wandered off?"

"We're not going very far," Eda insisted.

Lucy sniffed. "I cannot stand cold water."

"It won't kill you to dip your toes in the river," Eda said.

Lucy gave her a threatening look but did not say a word.

"How will we catch fish?" Belle demanded. "Don't fishermen use special poles and hooks and such? We don't have anything like that."

"I would hate to catch nothing more than a bad chill," Lucy added.

Eda had to think. "We'll use Ma's sewing basket."

"What about the spools of thread? What about the scissors? They'll float away," Lucy said.

"Ma won't like that," Belle said.

Again Eda paid no attention to her sisters' protests. She crept into the cabin, found the sewing basket, and dumped its contents on the floor. She hurried outside, smiling broadly. "Follow me," she said and walked to the river's edge. For once, her sisters did just what she told them.

The river tumbled around boulders and rushed headlong over fallen branches. It splashed and played and sang. The river chattered happily, even though the gulch was dark and narrow and often seemed forbidding. On either side, the walls of rock rose nearly straight up, keeping out the sunlight.

Eda slipped off her shoes and socks. She rolled her skirt up around her waist.

Belle did the same. "I'm glad no one back home can see me now," she said. "I look ridiculous."

"Do you think this is safe?" Lucy demanded. She took off her shoes but refused to remove her stockings.

"Shh!" Eda hissed. "You'll scare the fish." She and Belle waded into a still pool. The water felt numbingly cold. Belle made a face but did not speak. Carefully, Eda lowered the sewing basket into the water. A beautiful speckled trout swam in lazy circles near her ankles. Eda dared not move. She dared not breathe.

"Teeth!" Belle shrieked. "It has teeth!"

The fish twisted and sped out of sight.

"You've scared it away!" Eda scowled at her sister. "Trout don't bite."

Belle flushed with embarrassment. "How do you know?"

"Perhaps if we work together we can corner it," Lucy suggested, her head swathed in a shawl. She sloshed into the water up to her ankles, then quickly retreated to shore. "That is awful cold. Too cold for me."

"Please shut up, both of you," Eda demanded.

"Don't be rude, Eda," Belle said. "Let me try." She grabbed the basket from Eda and dipped it into the water. The fish swam close. "He bit me!" She tossed the basket into the water and rushed pell-mell toward dry land. "He bit me!"

Before Eda could retrieve the basket, the current caught it and carried it down the river.

"The basket! Get it, Eda," Lucy called to her.

Eda plunged through the water, over the slippery round rocks. She stubbed her toe and slipped. She had no feeling left in her feet. The basket was lodged between two boulders. She had to get it before it was swept away by the current. So intent was Eda on retrieving the basket that she did not hear her sisters shout. She did not notice what stood between the trees, watching her.

She bent over, breathless and freezing. With two fingers she picked up the basket. When she looked up, she saw something. At first she thought it might be a deer in the forest. But as she stared, she saw that it was a pale, skinny boy. His movements were quick and nervous.

Eda rubbed her eyes, wondering if she was having a dream or a vision. It seemed like ages since she'd seen or talked to anyone besides her parents and her sisters. "Hello?" Eda called. "Who are you?"

The boy stared in surprise, frozen like an elk in lantern light. His eyes were wide-set and dark. He carried a string of fish in one hand. He lifted the fish and signaled to Eda, but his startled expression did not change. He took a few steps closer.

Eda threw the basket and splashed to shore. As soon as she did, the boy hooked the fish to a low tree branch and scrambled out of sight.

"Come back!" Eda cried, chasing him. Who was he? Where was he going? Tree branches whipped her face and clung to her dress, but she kept running. The trees were dark. She stopped running and stood in the shadows, her heart pounding. This was as far away from the cabin as she had ever traveled alone.

She looked around. Where had he gone? Somewhere ahead of her she heard the crash of underbrush. "Hello? Wait!" she cried. She darted farther ahead, but when she arrived at the place she thought she had heard the noise, she found only a squirrel staring at her with dark beady eyes.

Eda watched the squirrel with the familiar dark eyes scamper away. The sight made her stop. What if the boy was a shape-shifter, like the ones Dick had described? What if he had transformed himself into a squirrel just to confuse her?

She turned and stumbled. Everything looked confusing from this direction—fallen branches, broken limbs. Where was the cabin? She tried to remember which way she had walked but everything looked the same. This way? No, this. She tripped but kept going until finally she saw the tumble-down roof, and then there were the familiar faces of her sisters, who looked angry and worried at the same time.

"Why did you run off like that?" Lucy demanded with the soggy sewing basket under one arm.

"You should see yourself," Belle said. "Your dress is ripped. Your face is filthy."

"A boy," Eda said breathlessly. "I was following a boy through the trees. Did you see him?"

Belle looked at Lucy with one eyebrow raised. Then she examined Eda closely. "Are you all right?"

"He hung some fish on a tree—right over there." Eda hurried to the tree near the river.

Hooked to a low branch were the fish. "You see," she said triumphantly, "I was right. The boy was real. He left these for us."

"Should we eat them?" Lucy asked doubtfully.

"I don't see why not," Belle said. "I'm hungry enough to eat just about anything."

Eda and her sisters built a small fire near the bank of the river. Eda wished she knew how to cook. "What do we do first?" she asked.

Belle and Lucy shrugged. "We could use a fork and hold it over the fire the way Dick cooked that piece of venison," Belle suggested.

The dead fish seemed to stare at Eda accusingly as she tried to poke it with a fork. She closed her eyes and stabbed. Gingerly, she held the impaled fish over the roaring flames.

"It smells like it's cooking," Belle said encouragingly.

The fish smoked, sizzled, and fell into the flames. Eda managed to scoop it out, but her dress nearly caught fire.

"Here we go. Get some plates," Eda said. Belle handed her a plate. Eda unceremoniously dumped the ash-flecked fish on the plate. "It looks delicious!" she said.

The girls sat on rocks, the fish between them.

They used their fingers and a knife to peel away the shriveled skin. Hungrily, they tore the fish apart and pulled away bones. They quickly ate the partly raw, partly burned fish. For the first time in a week, Eda felt full.

They cooked and ate the remaining fish the same way, saving a portion for their mother.

"Look, Ma," Belle announced, presenting Ma with a rare treat—supper served in bed. "Some lovely trout."

Ma sat up with a coverlet wrapped around her shoulders. "Where did it come from? Lucy, I told you not to go near the water."

"We didn't catch this fish," Belle said truthfully. "Some boy did. Eda saw him."

Ma sniffed the fish. "It smells all right. But why did he give it away?" she asked suspiciously.

Eda shrugged. "Maybe to be neighborly."

Ma nibbled a little piece. "I didn't know we had any neighbors. Did you thank him properly?"

"I didn't get a chance," Eda said. "I tried to follow him, but he ran away."

"A nicely brought up young man shouldn't behave like that," Ma said. "Well, if he comes back, we shall thank him properly and then perhaps we'll have the opportunity to meet his family."

For the first time in ever so long, Eda saw her mother smile. Eda wondered if she longed for company, too.

That night Eda sat inside the cabin and wrote in her journal:

August 4

Our house has but one room in it and that is now full. In one corner stands a rude concern made for a bedstead. In another stands our stove. We found a table here, with four rough shelves fastened to the legs, answering for a cupboard. Our melodeon, a rocking chair, three boxes, and a few three-legged stools make up the rest of our furniture. Two dripping pans and a spider, or small frying pan, hang against the log wall. These answer for pictures.

She paused. Back home, they'd had a proper parlor with expensive fifteen-dollar varnished lithographs on the wall above the horsehair sofa. When Eda shut her eyes, she could still see the lithograph of the girl washed up on the island in a tempestuous storm. It was such a lonely, heart-breaking scene. Eda had never understood why her mother found it so appealing, except that Mrs. Osborne down the street had one, too, and Ma always tried to copy whatever decorations Helen Osborne could afford.

Eda looked up at the dingy cabin wall and the hanging pans. By flickering lantern light she imagined that they were famous portraits. She wrote:

Although the background is rather dark, the features of Bonapart are distinctly visible in one pan, Daniel Boon the hermit in another.

All her life Eda had been made aware of the importance of her family's many possessions. Ma had constantly reminded Eda and her sisters that it was this wealth of leather-bound books, gleaming marble-topped tables, sentimental plaster sculptures, rosewood desks, wall-to-wall Brussels carpets, ornately framed mirrors, and doilies and pillows that set them apart and made them vastly superior to their less affluent neighbors and their poor relations. Ma took great delight in cramming as many expensive items as possible into the parlor. "Providing there is space to move about without knocking over the furniture," Ma always said, mouthing advice she had read in a ladies' magazine, "there is hardly likely to be too much in any room."

It had nearly broken Ma's heart when their many precious knickknacks were sold in a humiliating public auction conducted by cruel men from the bank. Pa said they needed every cent to make the journey west to Colorado and set themselves up in a mining claim. "As soon as I strike it rich, you can buy anything you want," he promised. This seemed to soothe Ma. But it did not temper Belle's outrage.

"I will not be parted with my wardrobe," she announced. "A woman is nothing without fine clothes." Belle had spent a great deal of time packing three satin dresses with flounced skirts and her best crinoline petticoat. Instead of taking all three of her favorite gay frilly hats with the feathers and artificial flowers, she took only one and felt it a great sacrifice.

Lucy had been less difficult about the reduction in their material possessions. Now that she had decided she would most likely be an old maid all her life, she announced that she had very little need for opera cloaks or fancy hats decorated with stuffed birds. Piously, she asked only to take along her prayer book, her ivory-handled walking stick, a somber gray bonnet, and one equally dull dress to wear to church.

Eda's needs were even simpler. Unlike Belle, Eda was not arrestingly pretty. Yet unlike Lucy, Eda burned with ambition. Eda was convinced that she would one day escape the clutches of her mother and her critical older sisters on the basis of her ability to write. She insisted on packing her palm-sized secret journal and a box of new pencils. She believed these would be the instruments of her salvation.

Being in quite a practical mood I have composed a hymn addressed to the mother bird I saw this afternoon perched over my head in the woods. I will note down the words for fear I shall forget it:

> *As wandered forth mid shrub and tree*
> *In quest of something new to see*

There, I have forgotten all the rest, but never mind. I won't let Belle know it and I can have the good of thinking that I did compose a long hymn.

Tomorrow I go to find the mysterious boy who brought us the fish.

Chapter 5

The next day was Sunday. Eda knew that Ma and her sisters would spend the entire day reading Scripture and sitting still and behaving just as they did when they lived in Pennsylvania. The only difference, of course, was that there was no church, no neighbors, no Sunday school. Nevertheless, Ma, Lucy, and Belle put on their best gowns and sat primly atop packing cases as if they were seated on chairs in their parlor.

The day was warm and sunny and cloudless, and Eda felt even more restless than usual. After a brief midmorning meal of crackers and sardines,

Ma and her sisters took a nap. Eda knew this was a perfect time for her to make an escape.

She hurried through the woods to the place where she had first seen the wonderful stranger. There was something thrilling about finally leaving the confines of the cabin without telling anyone. Ma had warned her and her sisters never to leave the area because of bears, mountain lions, Indians, and guerrillas. Since they had yet to see any of these things, Eda was eager to go exploring.

The appearance of the boy meant that somewhere nearby there must be a family—or perhaps a larger group of people. She knew that Ma would be furious when she found out she'd disobeyed, but Eda needed to practice going against the wishes of her mother if she planned to escape to college far, far away. College, Ma said, gave proper young women dangerous ideas that ruined their impressionable minds. "Or if I decide instead to become a famous playwright," Eda reasoned, "I must practice taking down my impressions of the people I meet. I cannot meet any new people if I never leave home."

Eventually Eda found what appeared to be a trail through the woods. This made her progress easier. Every so often she looked around to memorize the way she had come. When the trail forked, she stopped. Large, rude gray birds darted overhead. One swooped down to inspect her.

"Hello!" she cried. "Which way?"

The bird cocked its head and looked at her with keen black eyes. It flapped its wings and flew off. She followed the bird down the path that led to her right. Wind moved the tops of the pine trees. Small striped ground squirrels scampered along branches. The path wound past enormous boulders that reminded Eda of great gray eggs. She felt it was harder and harder to walk as the path became steeper. But not once did she consider giving up and going home. She was on an adventure.

Little by little the trees began to disappear and full sunlight flooded the path. Eda was delighted to discover that she had reached the top of a rocky ridge and could see far beyond the gulch below her. Happily she perched on a rock and took out her journal:

I feel tingly and gloriously alive! The sky is full of wondrous clouds that look like mansions or like angels on bucking horses. I can see mountains with names I don't know. Everything smells of dust and sage and a kind of animal smell, too. And all together, the smell of the sun on all of it—oh, rapture! I hope I never forget the feeling I have at the top of this ridge.

She closed her journal, stood up, and continued walking. The path took a turn and began to descend into a narrow valley. Eda stopped. She sniffed the air. Now she could smell woodsmoke. A dog barked. She walked faster.

Down in the hollow, half hidden by trees, was the strangest house Eda had ever seen. The roof glinted bright silver in the sunlight. As she came closer, she realized it was entirely made from flattened tin cans overlapped and nailed in place. After a few more steps, she felt a twinge of fear. All around the cabin's trampled yard were strange contraptions that whirled and sighed in the wind.

Twang-thump-twang-wham! The machines twirled every which way the wind blew. As she stared, she recognized the shapes of people and animals. There were comical people hammered from tin cans and pieces of wagon wheels and bits of bent metal. One was of a man with his arms spiraling around and around just out of reach of a fat metal pig that bucked and jumped. Another was of a woman whose legs peeked out from beneath her dress as she jumped over fences, back and forth, in a very unladylike way.

Eda had never seen such an odd collection of waltzing bits of metal. Who had made these? Had she stumbled upon some dangerous crazy person's workshop? For several moments she could not think what to do. She simply stood in the yard and listened to the metallic music.

"The whirlabouts ain't for sale," a voice said.

Eda looked up, startled, and saw the pale boy who had brought the fish. Seeing him close up, she guessed he was nine or ten years old. His hair was the color of corn tassels in August, and the expression in his eyes was just as perplexed as it had been the first time she saw him. He was barefoot, and his legs looked as if they had never been washed. A piece of rope held up his short, ragged pants. One of his sleeves was missing.

"Who made these things?" Eda asked, unable to think of anything else to say.

"Ulysses," the boy replied impatiently. Then he disappeared inside the house.

What a strange, unfriendly person! And who in the world was Ulysses? Eda took a few steps closer to the cabin. She had come all this long way and she had not even thanked the barefoot boy for the fish. Bravely she knocked on the door.

No answer.

She heard laughter and singing inside the cabin. She knocked again.

The door was flung open. Staring up at her was a small girl of five or six dressed completely in white mosquito netting. She carried a long stick with a glittering paper star at one end. Her scruffy blond hair was encircled by a wreath of flowers. She waved Eda inside with her star. Awkwardly, Eda took a step into the darkened cabin.

"Hello," Eda mumbled. "My name is Eda and I've come to—"

"You're late. The show's started. Sit down," the little girl commanded. She had a low, rough grown-up voice. Clearly, she was accustomed to being obeyed.

There wasn't time for Eda to follow Ma's advice to introduce herself formally. She took a seat on a barrel. As her eyes became used to the darkness, she saw at the end of the cabin a curtain hanging from the ceiling. It appeared to be made from an old piece of wagon canvas. Sitting in front of the canvas were several people. She could not see who they were in the darkness. Two were rather large; the rest were small. The small ones fidgeted, turned, and looked at her with curious, angry expressions that made her wonder if she had done something very rude.

Eda watched, amazed, as a lantern was lit, the curtain parted, and the little girl with the star walked out to face the audience. She clasped her hands together, nodded toward someone else hidden in the darkness, and sang sweetly:

> *"Buffalo gals, won't you come out tonight,*
> *Won't you come out tonight, won't you*
> *   come out tonight?*
> *Buffalo gals, won't you come out tonight*
> *And dance by the light of the moon?"*

The little girl looked around. She gestured emphatically, then cleared her throat and sang again:

> *"And dance by the light of the* mooooon.*"*

The fish boy appeared, carrying a stick with a bright white-painted circle at one end. He walked across the stage with the moon and grinned triumphantly.

The audience clapped. Eda clapped, too. The girl with the star bowed and left the stage. The boy remained onstage. He set down the moon and began juggling twirling pie pans. He blushed when he dropped two. But the audience did not seem to mind. He was applauded roundly. The curtain swept shut.

Someone swung open the door, and the room was flooded with sunlight. "A remarkable performance," a man's deep voice said.

"Intermission, everyone!" a child shouted.

Three children and a dirty baby scuttled fast as crabs out the door. None of them seemed the least bit disturbed that Eda, a complete stranger, was watching them with her mouth agape. She looked around and discovered that she was seated in a home unlike any she had ever seen before. Bunches of dried flowers hung from the ceiling. Bowls of half-eaten stew still sat on the table, which was pushed against the wall. The beds were unmade. A skinny rooster perched on one of the chairs eating a piece of pie. In the corner was a cradle stuffed with hay. Something scratched and scrambled inside.

Eda crept closer for a better look.

"Marmots bite," warned an older girl with dirty blond braids. She looked to be perhaps eight years old. She was dressed in a purple cape. "Don't put your hand in 'less you want him to get the deadwood in you."

"Deadwood?" Eda asked.

The girl crossed her scabby arms in front of her. " 'Less you want him to put you in a bad way."

"I see," Eda said. "No, of course I don't want *that.*" She watched the burrowing furry brown animal, which was no bigger than the prairie dogs she had seen on the plains. She wondered where the baby slept.

"Come on out here, Wyoming!" a man's voice called. Eda followed the girl outdoors. "Greetings!" said a tall man with a long, narrow face. He wore a long pointy hat painted with stars.

"Pleased to make your acquaintance. My name is Eda," she said. Somehow she couldn't keep herself from staring impolitely at the paper cone that he had slipped over his nose.

"What did you think of the performance?"

asked a woman with an open, friendly face. She was amazingly plump and wore a bright pink short skirt, slippers with faded pink ribbons tied around her ankles, and black stockings.

Eda was so perplexed by the woman's shockingly short skirt that she didn't know what to say. Ladies never wore such unseemly outfits. Ladies, Ma said, always kept their legs and arms covered.

"It was a . . . a wonderful show," Eda stammered. Secretly she wondered if the woman was one of the totally depraved creatures that Ma and her sisters had warned her about.

"Since you liked it so much, I know you'll stay for the second act. We have a special finale I think you'll enjoy." The woman beamed at Eda, then took her arm and led her around the back of the cabin. There was no stage set up in this area, just a clothesline strung between two tall pine trees. A ladder leaned against one of the trees. "Please, can we have some refreshments for our guest?"

The other children were gobbling bright red raspberries from a big washbasin. Their faces were smeared with the juice. The woman in the slippers scooped a handful of berries for Eda.

"Where are my manners? We have not introduced ourselves. This is Ulysses."

The gentleman who made the whirlabouts removed his pointy nose and bowed.

"These are my children," she said, pointing at the two boys, two girls, and a baby who paid no attention to Eda. "That one is named Nebraska. He's the one who brought you the fish. That girl's Wyoming. The other boy is Kansas. The little one in wings is Colorado, and the baby chewing on the shoe, his name is California."

"Such unusual names," Eda said. She sidestepped just in time to avoid a collision with Nebraska, who was pelting Colorado with pinecones.

Kansas knocked Wyoming to the ground and held her in a headlock. "Only let me get ahold of your beggarly carcass once," Wyoming howled, "and I will use you up so small that you won't be seen no more."

Their mother seemed undisturbed by the wild scrambling and vicious hair-pulling. "And surely you've heard of me," she continued. "Primrose of the West. Of course I sometimes was called Miss Ella LaRue. Nice ring to it, don't you think? You can call me Edith."

Eda nodded. She couldn't imagine addressing

this grown-up stranger in tights by her first name. It didn't seem proper, even though Edith was no shivering, frail, homegrown little thistle, like the neighbor ladies back home, whom Eda addressed as Miss or Missus. Edith was a big woman with a big voice and an even bigger laugh.

"Let me show you my clippings," Edith said. "Where are my clippings, Ulysses?"

Ulysses shrugged. He was busy twisting a piece of twine around a horseshoe and a rusty buckle attached to the top of one of the whirlabouts.

Edith hurried inside the cabin and came out with a sheaf of yellowed, curled newspapers. "See here? My act in Denver. That's the most recent. I crossed the street, from the brick building on the corner of D and Union to the balcony of the opera house. About two thousand people saw me in my short frock, tights, and trunks." She searched Eda's face as if to check if Eda was properly impressed. "Oh, it was a beautiful night! Big round moon overhead and two bonfires set up on the streets. It was my crowning glory."

"You crossed the . . . the street," Eda stammered, "and all those people came to watch?"

Edith hooted and slapped her thigh. "I crossed

the street on a *tightrope,* my dear! On a tightrope forty feet above the ground!"

Eda smiled politely. She glanced at the article and read that Edith had crossed over waterfalls, horse corrals, streams, and orchards on tightropes.

"I was a large figure," Edith said with pride. "Immense, really. That night in Denver I met Ulysses. He photographed me. He was the finest photographer on the front range. I just love him to pieces. Don't I, Ulysses?"

Ulysses looked up at Edith bashfully. She gave him a loud kiss on his skinny cheek. Eda glanced away shyly. She wasn't accustomed to being around families who said affectionate things aloud and gave each other noisy, sloppy kisses. Her parents never did such things. She was sure of that.

"Places! Places, everyone!" Edith shouted.

Colorado, the little girl with the star, and her feisty seven-year-old brother Kansas grabbed poles and battered silk parasols. They scrambled up the ladder as fast as mice up a corncrib. Fearlessly they tiptoed out onto the tightrope. They waved their sticks and parasols, walked back and forth, and met right in the middle of the rope. The rope began to sway.

"Watch your posture!" Edith shouted. "Chins! Chins! Remember your chins!"

Eda watched breathlessly. She dared not speak. The rope was only six or eight feet off the ground, but Colorado and Kansas looked very small and fragile up there without any net beneath them. The two tiny tightrope walkers exchanged parasols, made dainty bows, and quick as spiders made their way back to the trees and ladders at either end.

Edith and Ulysses clapped loudly. Wyoming whistled and stomped. "How do you like that?" Edith said. "They didn't fall once. Next time we're going to add some juggling."

"What about my idea?" Kansas piped up.

"Flaming torches?" his mother replied. "I don't know. You're a bit young."

Kansas scowled. "Long as I don't set my hair on fire like that other time."

"I still like my wheelbarrow plan," said Nebraska. "All we got to do is find a bear cub and dress it up and put it in the wheelbarrow. We'll call him the Blood-sweating Behemoth of the Holy Writ."

"What does that mean?" Kansas demanded. He stood on one leg and rubbed his dirty knee with his foot.

"Dunno. I just like the sound of the words," Nebraska said and gave his brother a shove.

"How you going to get a bear to sit in a wheelbarrow?" Wyoming piped up. She twirled one of her dirty braids between her fingers. "What if he falls into the audience and his mother comes a-looking for him?"

"We'll think about it, then vote," Edith said. "Show's over for now!"

Eda felt surprised that children had voting rights. In her family Pa decided everything.

"We do this every Sunday," Edith said proudly.

"You don't observe Sabbath?" Eda asked, amazed. She had never met anyone who didn't say prayers or at least attend services every Sunday.

"We've never been to church," Edith replied.

Eda found this hard to believe. "When you were married, surely you—"

"We wasn't ever married," Edith said cheerfully.

Dumbstruck, Eda watched the five children scamper around the yard. *Then where did all these children come from?* she wondered.

"Say," Edith said with enthusiasm, "maybe you'd like to learn to walk a tightrope. I bet you'd be very good at it. I can tell by the way you stand. All you need is steady nerves."

Eda felt her face flush clear to her ears. "I'm afraid of heights," she murmured. She'd never admitted this to anyone before.

"No need to be embarrassed. Walking a tightrope is no more difficult than walking down the street," Edith said. "You just have to keep your eyes steady and your body balanced." She made a line in the dirt with a broomstick. "Let's see you walk that line."

Eda took a deep breath. All the children were studying her. How ridiculous to walk on a line and humiliate herself in front of strangers! What if they made fun of her?

"Well, are you going to walk it or not?" Colorado demanded.

Eda smiled weakly. She did not wish to look like a coward. Using the broom to keep her balance, she walked toe to heel along the line. When she reached the end, Colorado burst into rowdy applause. "You see? It ain't hard."

Eda smiled and felt grateful.

"You're a talented girl," Edith said. "What else can you do?"

Eda dug her hands in her pockets. Colorado and the other children edged closer. "Well, I'm actually a writer," Eda said shyly.

"Excellent!" Edith exclaimed. "Did you hear that, Ulysses? We have a writer in our midst. What do you write?"

Eda felt too tongue-tied to speak.

"Murder mysteries?" Edith asked.

Eda shook her head.

"Song lyrics?"

Eda shook her head again, then said finally, "I'm working on a play."

"Ulysses! Children!" Edith exclaimed with delight. "Gather 'round. Our prayers have been answered. We've found exactly what we need—a playwright."

Colorado looked at Eda suspiciously. "What kind of plays do you write?"

"We want something with blood and guts and glory," Kansas announced. "I'm good at death scenes. You want to see me die?" Before Eda could answer, he clutched his throat and rolled around in the dust, gasping and gagging.

"You got some comic songs in your show?"

demanded Wyoming, waving her hand in Eda's face.

"What about a trapeze act?" Nebraska asked.

"Indian stories—that's what I like," Kansas said. He ran around in a circle in a wild war dance.

"Actually," Eda said, desperate to come up with something—anything, "there is an Indian story. I thought it up after we studied a poem by Longfellow in school."

"You have to go to school?" Nebraska said scornfully.

"I think I've heard of this Longfellow," Edith said. "He had a minstrel show in Chicago."

"Is your play one of them massacre stories? Does anybody get burned at the stake?" Kansas demanded. He licked his lips.

"Well, tell us about it. Aren't you going to tell us the story?" Nebraska demanded. "We got to hear it first to know if we want to do it. Ain't that right, Ulysses?"

Ulysses nodded.

All faces turned to Eda. There was no escape. She took a deep breath. "I'm imagining a forest beside a lake. That's the setting. And there's this brave little warrior boy. His name is Hiawatha.

He has these adventures, and he grows up and—"

"I'm Hiawatha!" Nebraska interrupted. "I'm the biggest."

"She said he's little in the beginning," Kansas reminded him. "We should put California in the first act. He's a baby."

Wyoming rolled her eyes. "California eats scenery, and he screams too much."

"What about costumes? We need costumes," Colorado announced. She pulled an old chest out of the house and dragged it into the yard. It was filled with a riot of color—dresses and pants and outfits of every shape and size. Instantly the children scrambled to grab something to wear— scarves, feathers, beads. Colorado seemed to take special delight in decorating the others' faces with purple chalk stripes.

"There. How do we look?" Wyoming said.

Eda felt dizzy. Everything was happening so quickly. "I . . . I haven't finished writing the play yet. There's no script. It's still in my head. I didn't realize you meant to act it out today."

"We can't wait around forever, you know. You say you've got a play," Nebraska said. "It's in your head, ain't it? So tell it."

Eda tapped her chin with her finger. No one had ever performed one of her plays before. She suddenly had a delicious sense of pleasure and power in knowing that her most fantastic make-believe could actually come to life. "We've got to have a green-and-yellow vision."

"What's that?" Nevada demanded.

"It's what Hiawatha's dreaming," Eda explained.

"A nightmare?" Kansas said eagerly. "I'd like to play that role."

"It's more of a vision than a nightmare, really," Eda said. She felt amazed at how easy it was to describe her thoughts and have them instantly acted upon. No one thought her odd. No one questioned what she had created. And best of all, none of the grown-ups interfered.

"I know exactly what Green and Yellow Vision looks like," Wyoming said. She ran inside their cabin and came out with a flour sack, which she quickly tore, then decorated with part of a broken yellow parasol. She slipped this over her head. "How do I look?"

"Perfect," Eda said, smiling. "And this is how it begins: 'By the shores of Gitche Gumee, By the shining Big-Sea-Water, Stood the wigwam of Nokomis, Daughter of the Moon Nokomis.'"

The rest of the afternoon disappeared so quickly in performing the production that Eda was amazed to realize that the sun was beginning to set. "I've got to go home," she said. The thought of walking through the darkness terrified her.

"Nebraska," Edith ordered, "you take her home. You know the way."

Nebraska grumbled that he really didn't want to. He was having too much fun pretending to be Hiawatha. But he went anyway. Eda was glad he came along, even though he was completely silent. It was so dark that she could barely see her hand in front of her face by the time they came to the gulch.

"Thanks for giving us the fish," Eda told him when they reached the clearing.

Nebraska shrugged and disappeared. Eda tiptoed toward the cabin. She could see lantern light blazing on the other side of the doorway. Inside, her sisters and mother sat quietly knitting and sewing. China cups of tea sat on the packing crate they used as a table. The cabin was so quiet, so orderly. The beds were made, the floor swept. Dinner dishes had been washed and dried. There were no footprints of muddy pets or handprints of sticky children anywhere.

"Where have you been?" Belle demanded when she saw Eda in the doorway. "We have been worried sick."

"You know you're not supposed to wander off," Ma scolded. "A barbarous attack might have befallen you. You are an inconsiderate child to make us worry so."

"I'm sorry," Eda mumbled. "I went to visit the family of the boy who gave us the fish. I lost track of time, I guess."

"A proper caller never stays longer than three-quarters of an hour," Ma reminded her. "What manner of people were they?"

Eda had to think. She had never met anyone like Ulysses, Edith, and the children. She doubted her mother had, either. "They are a large family," Eda said slowly, "with five children."

Ma raised an eyebrow. "I should say. Well, it's difficult to imagine a proper Christian family so far from civilization. What is their last name?"

Again Eda was stumped.

Ma raised her other eyebrow in hopeful anticipation.

"LaRue," Eda said, recalling one of the names Edith had given.

"LaRue? Sounds French. I wonder if they are related to the LaRue family of New York."

Eda shook her head. "I don't think so. They named their children Nebraska, Colorado, Kansas, Wyoming, and California."

Ma frowned. "Those are not proper Christian names! Where are these LaRues from?"

Eda paused to consider. She had never thought to ask that question. "I don't know," she admitted finally.

Her sisters looked at her disapprovingly.

Ma sighed with impatience. "What does Mr. LaRue do for a living?"

Eda felt puzzled. "You mean Ulysses? He makes whirlabouts."

"Whirlabouts?" Ma asked. "What are they?"

"Machines he invented that use wind for power."

Ma looked pleased. "An inventor! Perhaps he is well on his way to making his fortune."

"Not really. His machines aren't practical. They just make wind music."

"Wind music?" Ma said, furrowing her brow.

"Most extraordinary. Well, you may not visit these LaRues again unless you are properly chaperoned by one of us. Do I make myself clear?"

"Yes, ma'am," Eda said, glad not to have to answer any more questions.

Chapter 6

The next day Eda was bored to distraction while her sisters sat mending. She wished she could go back to Edith's house where there was plenty of excitement every minute. She knew there was no way she could escape the watchful eyes of her mother and sisters.

"Where do you think you're going?" Lucy demanded.

"Out into the yard for fresh air," Eda said. "Want to come with me, Belle?"

Belle nodded. She stood up and stretched. The two girls wandered down to the riverbank and sat on a rock. Belle glanced over one shoulder.

"I've started writing another newspaper column. Would you like to read it?"

Eda nodded eagerly. Belle handed her a piece of paper that said:

❧

August 7, 1864

Dear Readers:

Now we are situated in Young America Gulch. There are two mountains, covered with wormwood, within steps of the door on both sides of the house. Toward the upper end of the gulch is a grove of pine trees. Although we are out of sight of the snowy range yet the mountains around us are covered with perpetual snow. The ground is full of particles of yellow ore, which fools mistake for gold, but the wise have learned that all is not gold that glitters.

❧

Eda pointed to the last sentence. "This sounds like our family is rather foolish."

Belle reread the words and frowned. She

crossed this last part off and chewed on the end of her pencil. "I just can't think of another thing to say. I sat in the cabin all morning, but I couldn't come up with one more word. Maybe I'm not cut out for this writing business—"

Crack! A branch broke as if under a heavy weight. Eda jumped. "Indians!" she shouted.

Belle let out a warning cry. Eda raced inside the cabin close on her sister's heels.

"Hurry!" shouted Ma. She grabbed the rifle and thrust it into Belle's hands. Ma brandished an ax. Lucy hid under a coverlet.

Heavy footsteps came closer. "Can you see anything?" Ma demanded in a quavering voice.

Eda did not wish to risk sticking her face out the canvas-covered doorway. Instead she peeked through the wide cracks in the cabin wall. She saw a man on a horse, but he was not an Indian. He wore a proper black felt derby and a suit coat. "He might be a guerrilla," she whispered, not knowing if guerrillas wore derbies.

"Hello?" the man shouted. "Anyone home?"

"Who are you?" Belle demanded. She poked the barrel of the gun out the doorway and waved it about. "I am a crack shot. State your business."

The man nervously cleared his throat. "My

name is Mr. Dowdy, and I come from Cache Creek. Please put that rifle down. I mean no harm."

"Are you a guerrilla?" Eda demanded.

"No, ma'am," the man replied and chuckled in a way that Eda found most humiliating. "I am from the local school board."

Lucy crawled out from under the blanket. Belle parted the canvas door curtain so that she and her sisters could have a better look at Mr. Dowdy.

"I'm sorry to have frightened you," he said in an amiable voice. "Are you here alone?"

"Yes," Eda replied.

"No," Belle interrupted and gave her sister a sharp elbow in the ribs. "We expect our father and two hired men to return at any moment."

"I see," Mr. Dowdy said.

Eda looked at her sister in bewilderment. They had no idea when Pa would return.

"May I trouble you for some water?" Mr. Dowdy asked. "I am parched with thirst. Someone in the next valley told me that there were educated people here from Pennsylvania. I am from Philadelphia originally, and I thought I would pay a call. Perhaps you have heard of the

William Dowdys? We are a well-established family in the Philadelphia area."

At these words, Ma brightened considerably. She put down the ax and tried to smooth her rumpled dress. She pushed her daughters aside and stepped primly from behind the canvas door cover. "Please," she said, motioning in her most hospitable manner. "Mr. Dowdy, please excuse our trepidation. We are delighted to have such an honored guest. Won't you join us for tea?"

Mr. Dowdy lowered himself from his horse, which he tied to a tree. He was a short, spry man with a loping gait and dark, expressive eyebrows. His mustache was neatly trimmed, and he had an enormous gold watch chain in his neat vest pocket. Undoubtedly Mr. Dowdy was the best-dressed, best-smelling man they had laid eyes on since they crossed the Mississippi River. He smiled expansively as if they were already great friends. "I'd be delighted to share tea with you," he said and made a formal bow that clearly thrilled Ma.

Ma motioned to Belle to put the kettle on to boil. Eda cut the last of their brown bread into five equal slices. Lucy took a seat in the rocking chair, carefully concealing her misshapen foot beneath her long skirt.

"Are you going to help, Lucy, or are you just going to sit there like the queen of the May?" Eda hissed.

Lucy's jaw hardened into a stubborn line. She scowled at her youngest sister but did not reply.

"Well now, isn't this lovely?" Ma motioned for Mr. Dowdy to sit in the rocking chair.

He took a seat but politely waited till they were all served before he sipped his tea. "It makes me feel more than a little homesick to drink tea in such delightfully cultivated company," he said wistfully.

Ma blushed and refilled his cup. "It is our pleasure as well," she said. "In the wilderness it is easy to forget the finer things in life, I'm afraid."

Mr. Dowdy nodded. "You are absolutely correct. And that is in fact the reason for my visit. I have been living in Cache Creek, a community four miles from here. We are seeking the finer things in life for the children of our community."

Ma smiled generously at Eda and her sisters. "An admirable endeavor. My husband and I have always spared no expense to give our daughters the finest education money could buy."

"I am pleased to hear that," Mr. Dowdy said, "because I have been sent to engage a teacher.

And I hope that I might be able to entice one of your girls to Cache Creek to uplift the intellects of our young scholars."

For a moment no one spoke.

"How much are you paying?" Eda said. Her voice trembled with excitement.

"Seventy-five dollars a month, plus room and board," Mr. Dowdy said.

Eda could not help blurting, "I'd love to—"

"You are too young to go off by yourself, Harriet Adelle," Ma interrupted. Her face was flushed. She turned to Mr. Dowdy with a polite smile. "I'm afraid my daughters have always been carefully guarded and protected, Mr. Dowdy. They know nothing of the evils of the world. I cannot possibly—"

"But think of the money, Ma," Belle said. She clasped and unclasped her fine white hands. "Seventy-five dollars a month. We could certainly use the income."

Ma blushed an even deeper red. Revealing their lack of money in front of a person as fine as Mr. Dowdy caused her great embarrassment. Before Ma could speak, Belle continued, "I am seventeen years old, and I have passed through all grades of grammar school. I think I would make a fine teacher for your school, sir."

Mr. Dowdy looked at pretty Belle with obvious pleasure. "Have you ever taught school before?"

Belle shook her head but remained confident. "I am well skilled in the catechism of our church, and I am sure I can impart the love of learning."

Eda shot a curious glance at her sister. Belle had never seemed especially fond of either religion or books. Her interest ran more toward dresses, hairstyles, and the latest gossip. She had worked with soldiers in the hospitals back home mainly because she craved the companionship of the other young ladies who did charitable work for the war effort.

Eda felt angry to be denied this chance to escape from her family and demonstrate her abilities. *She* was the scholar, not Belle. *It's just not fair.*

Ma cleared her throat. Her fingers drummed the table. "Sir, may I speak with my daughters in private?"

"Certainly," Mr. Dowdy said. "I will be happy to remain outside while you discuss this opportunity."

As soon as he left, Ma's brow grew furrowed

with anger as she turned to Belle. "Women in the Derleth family do not demean themselves by working. Certainly no relative of mine has ever fallen so low as to teach school. I forbid you to take this position."

Belle sat up straight. She looked Ma square in the eye, absolutely unafraid. "That was all very well and good back in Pennsylvania. But you must have noticed that we have barely enough canned goods to keep us fed for another week. Since we do not know when Pa will return, and since none of us can hunt, we will soon need to buy more supplies from the nearest town. Without money we may soon face starvation."

Talk of economic concerns always offended Ma's fine sensibilities. She straightened her shoulders. "We are getting along just fine."

"Ma," Lucy said in a cajoling voice, "we are running low on supplies. I think you should let Belle take the job. Teaching is an admirable profession, and she may indeed save souls in this godforsaken place. I'm sure you agree, don't you, Eda?"

Eda doubted that Belle would save anyone's soul. At the same time she had to admit she was tired of being hungry. "I won't tell anyone back in Erie County," she promised.

Ma glanced at each of her daughters in turn. Finally she said in a resigned voice, "I shall ask your father—"

"If you wait to get Pa's permission, the job may be gone," Lucy reminded her. "We don't know how many other candidates Mr. Dowdy has interviewed."

Ma sighed. "All right, then, Belle. You may take the job."

Arrangements were soon made for Belle to leave the next day with Mr. Dowdy, and she went into a flurry of activity to get ready for her departure.

Eda watched her sister pack her things in both carpetbags. "You're not going miles away to Europe or something," she grumbled.

"At last I'll have someplace to wear my dresses!" Belle said with delight. "Isn't that wonderful? And with seventy-five dollars a month I may even have money left over to buy a new hat. Cache Creek will most certainly be a more exciting place than this dismal gulch."

"What about your splendid new career with the *North East Gazette*?" Eda asked.

"Oh, *that*," Belle said with a disparaging toss of her head, "I'll just write to Mr. Mead and tell him I'm quitting. Coming up with a column is boring, and no one cares what a writer wears when she works. Teaching is my splendid new career. I believe it will be far more glamorous."

Eda could not bring herself to feel glad about her fickle sister's change of plans. How could she so easily give up on writing? It seemed to Eda that Belle had all the luck and didn't even know it.

That night Eda wrote in her journal:

Belle leaves tomorrow. Good riddance. The worst of it is that I will be stuck here with sour old Lucy.

Chapter 7

August 8

Dear Dragonbreath,

I hope your are well. I am writing to tell you of our circumstances. No gold yet. But Pa says he has excellent prospects. He surprised us by appearing this morning, just in time to take Belle to Cache Creek on our little pony. She is full of ambition to commence her labors in school teaching. Pa brought the pony back and picked up several letters from friends at home. Lucy

had quite a feast reading her letters I think
she has more than her share. Please write
to me.

> Your friend,
> Eda

❧

The next four days passed slowly with no visitors, no letters, and no word from Belle or Pa.
Eda hoped that Edith might pay a call, but she
did not appear. The pony became Eda's favorite
companion. She brushed his shaggy coat and told
him all her troubles. Unlike Lucy and Ma, the
pony never complained.

One morning as Eda braided his mane with
flowers and leaves, Lucy shouted, "Eda!"

Eda kept brushing the pony.

"Eda! Do you hear me?"

Eda scowled. Lucy never called politely. She
never requested; she always commanded. Eda
had tried her best to obey her sister's orders, but
now she was growing so weary of Lucy that she
could barely stand the sound of her shrill voice.
Eda patted the pony and went into the cabin.
"What is it?" she said, scowling at her sister en-
throned on the rocking chair.

Lucy had a piece of paper on her lap. She was undoubtedly writing her daily letter to the pompous young minister back home—the one who filled the entire dusky church with his rolling cry of "Canst thou love Jesus?"

"My shawl," Lucy demanded. "Where is my shawl, Eda?"

"Probably in the same place you left it."

"I am feeling a chill. You know what happens when I get a chill."

Eda took a deep breath. "I am not your maid. Find the shawl yourself." She stomped out of the cabin and returned to the much more amiable pony.

"Ma!" Lucy wailed. "Ma!"

"Yes, dear," said Ma, who was outside in the yard struggling to wash a pair of stockings in a bucket. Gingerly she dipped the stockings into the cold water, rubbed them with soap, and held them between two fingers as if uncertain what to do next.

"Eda is doing it again!" Lucy complained.

Ma wrung out the soggy wool stockings and watched water dribble onto her shoe. Angrily she flung the offensive wet stockings into the dirt and headed for the house. "There! See if I care if you are clean or not."

"Ma, are you listening?" Lucy complained.

"I am not about to be a work-worn washerwoman."

"Ma!" Lucy said, increasing the pitch of her whine. "Eda refuses to help me. She absolutely refuses. And you know how I suffer."

"Your father is not being truthful, I'm afraid," Ma said. "I'm certain there's money somewhere that we could use to pay a laundress once a week."

"Ma! You're not listening. No one ever listens to me!" Lucy let out a terrific howl.

"My dear, this is quite intolerable!" Ma said with alarm and hurried to her daughter's side. "Eda!" she shouted out the door.

Eda shuffled inside the cabin and impassively watched her sister weep into their best coverlet.

"Eda, look what you've done. You should be ashamed," Ma said indignantly. Lucy sobbed louder. "You must assist your poor sister in all things."

"Every five minutes Lucy wants me to fetch her thimble or her pen or her reading glasses, even though they're just a few steps away," Eda complained. "She could get them herself."

"That's a lie!" Lucy said between sobs. "You refuse to help just to torment me. Belle would never be so cruel."

Eda put her hands on her hips. "You can walk, you know. You just don't—"

"Stop!" Ma said. She put her hand up. "My nerves cannot bear any more of this arguing. Eda, you *must* assist your sister. That's all there is to it."

Eda scowled. She wished to escape more than anything in the world. She would run through the woods. She would go and live with Edith and Ulysses. Anything was better than being trapped inside the cabin one more minute. Resolutely she turned on her heel, grabbed an empty bucket, and headed for the trees.

"Where do you think you're going?" Ma called after her. "You know you can't go into the woods. Pa said guerrillas stole three ponies near Cache Creek. Those men plunder and rob and do as much damage as they can. You must stay here where you are safe from those horrid Confederate sympathizers."

"I'm going . . ." Eda said and paused. She

thought of Nebraska and his brothers and sisters. They never had to ask permission to go anywhere. She recalled their happy, red-stained, sticky faces. Inspired, she announced, "I'm going to pick raspberries."

"Raspberries?" Ma said in astonishment. "Eda, come back here. Your sister needs company. I forbid you to leave."

Eda stopped, then said hastily, "Well then, Lucy can come with me."

There was a long pause, and finally Ma parted the covering in the doorway. She pressed her fingers to her temples the way she did whenever her nerves were bothering her. "I will repeat myself one last time. We are obliged to observe the utmost caution. No one can leave," she said. "And if you do not obey me, Harriet Adelle, you will have to answer to your father when he comes home."

Eda threw the bucket on the ground. She kicked rocks. She stomped to the riverbank and sat with her fists clenched. The only thing to do, she decided, was to wait until dark and then run away. She would escape from her mother and sister and this dull, prisonlike cabin forever.

But when darkness came, Eda heard the eerie

hooting of owls. The howling wind felt icy cold, and she knew that somewhere in the darkness mountain lions hunted for their supper, Indians lurked, and guerrillas lay in ambush. She hunched forward and stared at the fire inside the little stove's open door. Miserably, she scribbled in her journal:

Belle's the lucky one. Belle escaped.

All night Ma stayed awake, certain that the guerrillas Pa had warned them about would soon be upon them. As a result, she was just going to sleep as morning finally arrived. In the morning, Eda, who had slept soundly, felt remarkably better. She rubbed her eyes. As she walked out into the fragrant morning sunshine, she marveled at how much her moods were like the mountains. On one mountain, rain might be pouring in torrents while on the other the weather might be balmy. Sometimes her emotions were just as unpredictable.

Today, she decided, she would make a new start with her difficult sister. She would try to be kinder to Lucy, just as Belle had suggested. "Good morning," Eda said with a great smile when she saw her sister hobble out of the cabin in one of her rare encounters with fresh air. "It's going to be a beautiful day."

Lucy eyed Eda suspiciously as she sat on a stump and arranged the folds of her long dress. "What's so beautiful about it?"

"The sky, the sun, the clouds—everything. It's a perfect day to pick raspberries."

"You know what Ma said yesterday," Lucy said. "We're not to leave the cabin yard. It's too dangerous."

"I know a place where there are heaps and heaps of ripe, sweet berries. It's only a short distance from here. We'll be able to return at any moment we wish." Eda knew that Lucy liked nothing better than sweets. "The raspberries are as delicious as candy."

"You forget that I am unable to make such a long trip on foot," Lucy said grimly. "It is quite impossible."

"No, it's not. You can ride our pony. It would be a shame if Pa bought him and no one ever rode him anywhere. A terrible waste of good money."

Lucy did not speak. She seemed to be deep in thought. "I have never ridden a pony."

"Oh," said Eda with a chuckle, "he's so gentle, all you do is sit on his back. He knows exactly what to do. He never runs. He never canters. He's a slow old gentleman."

Eda led the pony close to Lucy, who stood and bravely patted the pony's head. When the pony nuzzled her arm, Lucy froze. "Will he bite?"

"No, he's just looking for a treat."

As if satisfied with her answer, Lucy relaxed a little.

"Give him this," Eda said, handing her sister a piece of cracker. "Hold your hand flat."

The pony gobbled the cracker from Lucy's hand.

"He likes you," Eda said.

"He does?"

Eda nodded. "He's a good judge of character. He knows that you're much more adventuresome than you let on."

"I am?"

"Yes," Eda said, warming to her sister's growing curiosity. "That's why you long to see something besides those four black sooty walls inside the cabin. After all, you need to have something to write to the Reverend Mr. Phillips about, don't you? He wants to read about your impressions of this place, so you'll have to get out of the gulch every now and again and take in the view."

"How do you know about the Reverend Mr. Phillips?" Lucy demanded.

Eda had to think fast. "I remember hearing him say, the Sunday before we left, that he hoped we'd all write to him." In truth, Eda had secretly read most of the young minister's sappy letters to her sister, mostly to see if he'd mentioned Dragonbreath. But the minister's narrative never strayed from the weather, the war, and the price of factory-made shoes, so Eda lost interest. Her sister's correspondence was far too dull to risk reading secretly. "Just think how pleased he'll be to hear that you are appreciating the wonders of nature," Eda added. She felt herself recoil even as she spoke the one phrase she remembered from the vapid minister's letters: "Wonders of nature."

"That *is* true," Lucy murmured.

"Well then, let's go. We'll leave a note for Mother in case we don't get back before she wakes," Eda said. While Lucy wrote a note for Ma, Eda collected some buckets and a blanket. In one bucket she placed some crackers and cheese, part of a sausage, and a knife. She had to overturn a box to provide Lucy with the step she needed to stand on one good leg while swinging the other over the pony's back.

"You're sure he won't buck?" Lucy demanded nervously.

"He'll do exactly as we tell him, won't you?" Eda gave the horse a sturdy pat. She took his reins and led him out of the cabin yard into the woods. They took the path that Eda had followed to Edith's. She had not really encountered any raspberries this way, but then again, she hadn't been looking.

"This is very pleasant," Lucy said. She looked all around her, but she held so tight to the saddle horn that her knuckles went white. "How far to the berry patch?"

"Soon," Eda said. She felt so glad to have escaped from the cabin and the watchful eye of Ma that she could have walked for miles and not felt the least bit tired.

Lucy also seemed unusually energized by their expedition. "Do you know what I miss most about Pennsylvania?" she said in a gay voice.

"What?" Eda asked, surprised by her sister's good mood.

"Frogs. I have not seen one frog since we've been in the mountains. And why is that?"

Eda smiled. "Perhaps it is too cold for them."

"Do you remember the time," Lucy said, "when you and your little friend Wallace had that great idea about the bullfrog?"

Good old Dragonbreath! How pleasant to think of him. "That frog lived under a board beneath the cherry tree in our yard. We used to lie on our stomachs and watch the frog flick his tongue out to catch flies. That cold spring Ma made us put on our coats and get off the grass. So I began to think that the old bullfrog was cold and needed clothes, too."

"How did you catch him?"

"A lard can with a cover." Eda chuckled. "Lucy, you were the one who cut out a jacket, a pair of pants, and a little sunbonnet and sewed them for us."

"I thought I was helping make clothes for your doll. You never did like dolls much. I thought you had taken a new civilized interest. How was I to know that I was actually making an outfit for a slimy frog?"

"We had an awful time squeezing him into the pants and shirt and sunbonnet."

Lucy giggled. "Ma was so indignant when she

saw what you'd done that she made you put that frog outside. Whatever happened to him?"

"We felt sorry for him, so we took off his handsome shirt and pants and sunbonnet and put him out on the board sidewalk, and he hopped away quite naked. We never saw him again." Eda laughed and laughed. So did Lucy. It felt wonderful to be laughing with her sister over something they both remembered.

The rest of the way up the mountain Lucy told fascinating stories about other things she remembered, stories that Eda had never heard before. "I recall everything perfectly about when you were a baby," Lucy said, "because I was seven when you were born."

"What did I look like?" Eda asked eagerly.

"You had pointy shriveled ears that looked like dried apricots."

Eda groaned. "What was my first sentence?"

" 'Kitty, get down.' "

"I was a bossy child," Eda said and laughed. "What else?"

"You liked to poke peas up your nose. And you were deathly afraid of feathers."

"Feathers?" Eda said indignantly. She didn't remember anything about feathers.

"That's right. They spooked you so much that I devised a clever plan: if I wanted you to stay out of my room, I simply placed a feather on the floor in plain sight from the open door; that was enough to keep you away."

Encouraged by Lucy's unusually talkative mood and by the fact that she was so much older, Eda decided to see if her sister could answer a question that had been bothering her ever since she'd left Edith's house. "Lucy, is it possible for people who are not married to have children?"

Lucy did not say anything. When Eda turned to look at her, she saw that her face had become even paler than usual. "Well," Lucy said hesitantly, "yes, I suppose."

"Then where do the children come from?" Eda blurted.

"It's not nice to ask about such things."

"Oh, please, Lucy," Eda pleaded, "surely you know. Won't you tell me?"

Lucy cleared her throat. "You've seen pictures and statues. You must have noticed that men . . . are made differently from women?"

"Yes," Eda said blankly: men wore trousers; women wore skirts.

"Well then . . ."

Eda could not think of a reply because she still did not understand.

"Then for heaven's sake don't ask me any more ridiculous questions," Lucy said. "I know you're not as ignorant as you pretend to be."

Eda sighed. The dreadful moment was over. Her shoulders slumped forward. Again she had been wrongly accused of stupidity for not knowing what she had been expressly forbidden to ask about, or even think about.

"Raspberries!" Lucy called and pointed.

On a nearby rise Eda saw low green leaves with the familiar jewellike berries. She had never before been so grateful to see raspberries. Now they could begin picking and stop talking about unpleasant topics.

Eda helped her sister dismount, and together they gathered fruit, nibbling as they went. Lucy was especially efficient about filling buckets while Eda ate nearly as many sweet juicy raspberries as she picked. The sun felt warm, the breeze was refreshing, and before long they forgot where they'd tethered the pony and left their picnic lunch.

"Where is he?" Lucy said, looking panic-stricken.

"We'll find him," Eda insisted. She hoisted the buckets and tried to retrace their steps. There were big logs and branches in the way, and the underbrush was thick and dry and crackled beneath their feet. Eda motioned to Lucy. "Over here!" Eda walked faster. She remembered something: bears liked berries; bears *loved* berries, in fact. What if they came upon a bear? They had no gun. They didn't even have a box of cayenne pepper.

"Are you sure it's this way?" Lucy called.

"Yes. I'm sure," Eda insisted. She glanced over her shoulder and watched her sister determinedly swing her lame leg over each fallen log while she hoisted her dress up out of the way of the prickly branches. Lucy's face was flushed, and she had that determined look Eda had seen before. The only difference was that this time she wasn't complaining. She wasn't trying to hide. She was just trying to keep up.

It was difficult enough for Eda to clamber over the fallen branches. What must it have been like for Lucy to do the same thing? Eda felt a grudging admiration for her sister.

Eda pushed through a thicket of low evergreens just in time to see a large black bear rambling away. He glanced at her as if to say, "Pray, to what race do you belong?" Then he rocked away on his enormous paws and vanished between the trees.

Eda could not move. "Good-bye," she whispered.

"Are you all right?" Lucy demanded when she finally caught up with Eda. "You look a little greenish."

"I'm fine," Eda said, glad that Lucy had not seen the bear. If she had, she probably would never have left the cabin again. "I think I ate too many berries."

Not far away they heard a familiar whinny. Eda hurried around a grove of trees and found the pony pawing the ground. She called to her sister. "I found him!"

"Good work, Eda," Lucy said with relief. "Now we can sit down and have our picnic."

And Eda smiled, savoring her sister's praise. She wondered if perhaps Lucy's heart was not as badly damaged as Belle had claimed.

Chapter

8

Harry pays a short visit. He relates that Indians are murdering the whites on the plains at a rapid rate. It is sad news but we hope they will soon be drawn to the Pacific and then pushed in. Heard also of brutal conduct of the Guerrillas. A band of 12 claiming to be Confederates attacked the stage last week a few miles below Fairplay on its way to Denver. Robbed the mail bag of its contents which was several thousand dollars in gold dust, and threatened to shoot the driver if he ever drove the stage again. A large group of miners have turned out to hunt for them and it is hoped they will be found.

"What are you writing?" Lucy demanded. She had come up so silently to Eda's favorite spot beside the river that Eda hadn't noticed her arrival.

"Nothing," Eda said. She quickly hid her journal beneath her apron.

"I'm not stupid. I can see you're writing something," Lucy said, sounding like her old peevish self. "Ma heard from Belle yesterday."

Eda jumped up from the rock where she had been sitting. She felt glad for the change of subject. "How is she?"

"Fine. Mr. Dowdy visited while we were gone on that silly berrying trip. He said she's doing an admirable job."

"Our trip wasn't silly," Eda said in a small hurt voice. She would never understand Lucy. One minute she was kind; the next, she was cruel. Eda was certain her sister had enjoyed herself, yet now she acted as if their adventure had been a lapse in her normally grown-up judgment. "I wish she'd come home to visit," Eda said, surprised to realize she missed Belle.

"I'm sure she's so busy she doesn't even think of us," Lucy grumbled and turned away.

Eda watched Lucy hobble toward the cabin. "You know, Lucy," she called after her, "nobody says you have to be miserable every minute."

Lucy stopped, turned, and looked back at her sister over her shoulder. Her face was flushed. "Thank you so much for your helpful advice," she replied angrily, then went to rejoin Ma in the cabin.

"Yoo-hoo!"

Eda started. *Guerrillas? Indians?* She jumped to her feet, ready to run. Suddenly a familiar figure emerged from among the trees.

"Anybody home?" Edith hollered. She was wearing oversize overalls and a man's slouch hat. Behind her came the wild cavorting and crashing and cartwheeling of Colorado, Nebraska, Kansas, Wyoming, and California. The children pushed their way through the underbrush carrying fishing poles and battered baskets and syrup tins. "Eda honey!" Edith exclaimed with delight. "We were hoping to find you here. We're going fishing. Want to come along?"

Eda could not think what to say. Colorado and the other children darted around the yard, tipping over crates, upending barrels, and inspecting casks. They crawled under the wagon with half a bucket of Eda's raspberries, eating as quickly as they could. Kansas made faces at Eda between the wheel spokes. "Well," Eda stammered, "I . . . I . . ."

Before she could finish her sentence, Ma awoke from her nap, stumbled to the doorway, and looked out. She rubbed her eyes and stared in horror as Wyoming and Kansas darted around her and into the cabin. "Come back here this instant!" she cried. "Don't you dare touch that melodeon!"

"A melodeon?" Edith said, her face brightening. "You didn't tell me you had a melodeon, Eda."

Eda smiled weakly. She heard all kinds of crashing and shrieks coming from inside the cabin. Lucy burst through the doorway, her hair disheveled. "They're scooping up marmalade with their hands!"

"Marmalade!" Edith said, licking her lips. "I haven't had such a treat in a goat's age."

Wheezing notes of the precious melodeon floated from the cabin.

Eda couldn't help herself. She smiled as she imagined the children jumping on the treadles to work the small reed organ's bellows.

Ma marched grimly toward Edith. "Your dirty children are playing *my* melodeon!"

"My little chickens play the harmonica, the Jew's harp, and the trumpet," Edith said, chuckling, "but don't none of them know how to play the melodeon. They've never had the opportunity till today. But I do appreciate the fact that you think they could learn. They—"

"*Remove* your children!" Ma barked. As soon as she let fly this command, she placed her fingertips on her temples as if her head throbbed dreadfully.

"Now, now," Edith murmured consolingly, "if you've got a bit of horseradish and some lemon and maybe a raw egg, I can make you a hair-of-the-dog mixture that will cure that morning-after headache. We all drink too much sometimes and—"

"I do not drink," Ma said through clenched teeth.

Edith clucked and shook her head. "Well then, maybe a good stiff drink is exactly what you need."

"Who are you?" Ma demanded. "And why are you invading my property?"

"Your property?" Edith said, inelegantly hooking her thumbs in her overall straps. "The truth is, this cabin still belongs to Amos Anderson, who never quit title on the place. This is what's called an abandoned claim, and you are what's called a squatter."

Ma sputtered but said nothing. It was clear that the term "squatter" had hit a nerve.

"As your friendly neighbors, we come paying a call," Edith continued, smiling as broadly as ever. She nodded toward Eda. "Your daughter here is a talented writer."

"Eda?" Ma muttered. "I don't think so."

"I even brought her some reading material," Edith continued, ignoring Ma's reaction. She took from her enormous pockets several old smoky pamphlets that looked as if they had been published long, long ago and had been hanging on a sooty cabin wall ever since. "You're welcome to borrow them, Eda. I've read these novel chapters at least a hundred times already."

"Thank you," Eda said, moved by Edith's generosity. She knew that Edith owned few books and she was deeply touched that she had shared anything so precious.

"My daughters do not read novels," Ma said primly. "I don't allow such rubbish in my home."

Edith scratched her armpit. "Well, what *do* you read?"

Ma's eyes narrowed. "Sermons. Books on horticulture. We do not allow our girls' minds to be defiled by silly novels."

Edith hooted. "This novel ain't silly. It's all true. Every word."

Eda quickly thanked Edith and took the precious greasy pages before Ma had an attack of the nerves.

"You know," Edith said confidentially to Ma, "your daughter Eda has great potential as a writer for the theater, or perhaps as a tightrope walker in the circus."

Outrage electrified Ma. "The theater? The circus? No Derleth has ever been involved in such loathsome professions. The very suggestion of such an idea offends me deeply, Mrs.— What is your name?"

"My stage name is Miss Ella LaRue," she said, then added in a chummy tone, "but you can call me Edith."

"Your *stage* name?" Ma replied. She wobbled, lowered herself onto a stump, and stared accusingly at Eda. "Harriet Adelle Hitchcock, you shock me. What possessed you to associate with this . . . this *actress?*"

"Look what we found!" Nebraska shouted. He leaped through the cabin doorway carrying a croquet mallet. Swiftly on his heels came his brother Kansas swinging a lawn tennis racket. They chased each other around the cabin several times.

"Ma!" Lucy wailed. She hobbled out of the cabin. "Stop them! They're painting themselves with my French face cream! They're dancing on the table!"

Edith calmly surveyed the chaos. It seemed to Eda that she looked with pride at the costuming of the pony, which Wyoming and Nevada had adorned with Lucy's somber church hat and Pa's silk necktie. "Such an eye for color!" Edith exclaimed. Then she turned to Ma. "When can *I* see your melodeon?"

"Never! Never! Never!" Ma shrieked.

"Well then, a cup of coffee would be nice," Edith said, still smiling. She rocked back on her heels.

"Coffee? You expect me to serve *you* coffee?"

"Tea would be just as neighborly if that's all you got," Edith said pleasantly. "Then we'll have a nice little fishing trip together. I think you'll enjoy fishing. You've never fished before, have you?"

Ma's shoulders slumped forward. "Certainly not."

"All the more reason to try. Your other daughter, too. What's your name, sweetheart?"

Lucy looked disturbed to have come under the scrutiny of Edith. "Hannah Lucille," she said in a dignified voice.

"Now, that's a mouthful!" Edith replied. "Got a nice sound to it, though."

"What happened to your leg?" Colorado inquired. She squatted on the ground and stared at Lucy's foot.

"Nothing," Lucy replied coldly. She tried to push away the inquisitive child who seemed determined to crawl under her dress. "Ma!" Lucy said plaintively.

"I always believe it's best to answer a child's questions truthfully." Edith winked broadly at Ma. "Saves on a lot of later ignorance and embarrassment, if you know what I mean."

"Make this little imp go away!" Lucy said, nearly bursting into tears.

Eda hurried to her sister's side. "Come on, Colorado. Why don't you help me get ready to go fishing?"

Colorado refused to budge. "Her foot don't look no worse than the time I fell in a badger hole and twisted my ankle," she said and sniffed. She turned to Lucy. "My ma's been struck by lightning and died twice. Why don't you come fishing with us?"

"Because," Lucy said, straightening herself up very prim and proper, "I cannot."

"You don't know how?" Colorado asked in disbelief.

Lucy nodded. "Now if you'll excuse me—"

"We can teach you easy. Nothing to it. If you fish at night, of course, you need a sharp spear and you build a fire. Fish is so stupid they come right to the surface and let you poke them easy. But we gots poles today. And Ma made lard sandwiches. You'll like lard sandwiches." Colorado took Lucy's hand and kept chattering and chattering. As if mesmerized, Lucy allowed herself to be led along by the little girl. Eda wondered if her sister had been entranced like some creature in *Grimm's Fairy-Tales*.

"You don't walk so poor," Colorado continued.

Kansas snorted. "Not no worse than that time I got stomped on by the mule."

"I'd sure like to see your foot," Nebraska said.

The children crowded around, not to be cruel, it seemed, but because they were truly curious.

"Give her some air. She's not your friend. She's mine," Colorado said fiercely. She gave one of her brothers an expert jab with her bony elbow. "Now, you just climb up on this little pony, Miss Lucy, and I'll lead you and you don't have to fear nothing."

Lucy gave a last desperate glance toward her mother, who seemed frozen to the spot beside the cabin as she watched the tide of dirty children retreat. "Stop!" Ma called. "You can take Eda but you may not take Lucy. She's far too delicate. Lucy, get down from that horse this instant."

Colorado seemed outraged by Ma's sudden intrusion on their fishing trip. "If she can't go, we'll all stay." She gestured at her brothers and sisters. Nebraska burped. Kansas picked his nose. California sucked marmalade from the front of his shirt. Wyoming chewed her fingernails and spit the little pieces on the ground.

Ma's face filled with disgust. She twisted a handkerchief as if she wasn't sure what to do.

"All right. If that's the only way to keep these barbarians from ruining everything I own, so be it. Lucy, you may accompany Eda, but you must be back before dark."

"Common sense. Common sense. That's what I always say," Edith told Ma with approval. "You made a sound choice. Well, we're off. Enjoy your afternoon."

Before Ma could answer, Edith heaved filthy California on to one hip. "See you later, Alligator," Colorado called.

"After while, Crocodile," Kansas finished the chant.

Lucy set off in the lead astride the pony, led by Colorado. Kansas, Wyoming, and Nebraska followed, all waving fishing rods and singing triumphantly:

> *"Buffalo gals, won't you come out tonight,*
> *Come out tonight, come out tonight?*
> *Buffalo gals, won't you come out tonight*
> *And dance by the light of the moon?"*

Eda was delighted. She had escaped. So had Lucy—thanks to a clever strategy by Colorado.

Chapter 9

August 14

There are very many speckled trout in Lake Creek half a mile from here. Lucy caught seven in a short time— much to her delight. She considers herself an expert now. Edith showed us how to cook fish. First we salted them. Then we skewered them whole on green sticks and toasted them in the low burning coals until they were cooked on both sides. We had to take care the fish didn't crumble or drop off the stick when they were nearly done. Delicious! Colorado braids Lucy's hair and tells us how her brother was kicked by a horse and was dead as a stick for three hours.

August 16

Too busy to write. Lucy rides the pony everywhere. We stage a blood and thunder show at Edith's called "Blackbeard at the Deadfall". Lucy sews pirate costumes. Wyoming explains where babies come from. She's five years younger than I am. What does she know? When I refuse to believe her disgusting story, she drags Edith into our discussion. Edith did not once say Not-Nice. She talked about love. I never assumed love was involved. To be perfectly honest, I am feeling rather relieved to finally hear the truth from a grown up. I am glad not to be ignorant any more—like Lucy, who believes in statues.

August 18

I have been down into the pit helping Pa and the men wash gold. Such hard work!

We were twenty feet below the surface of the ground. The water is brought two miles in a ditch to a reservoir and then let down into the pit through a gate with such a force that the ground caves off on both sides and as it runs through the flume the gold dust settles to the bottom and is caught in the riffles. The bottom of the boxes are then scraped out into pans and taken to the reservoir to be washed again and then as the dust is fine particles we use quick silver to save it. The flume extends to the Arkansaw River. The water makes such a noise that it is difficult to hear each other talk. When I go to call the men to dinner I am obliged to throw a stone down to make the men look up as they cannot hear me call. To get into the pit I am obliged to go down the bank to the river side and then climb over the rocks that have been dug out till I get back to where the men are at work. I had thought I would shorten my walk into the pit this afternoon by sliding down the bank onto a rock which projected from the side of the cave but as I struck it with too much force it gave way and carried me to the bottom and a plenty of sand following me. Not a very pleasant ride at the time but when the men found me I was not seriously hurt they had a hearty laugh at my expense.

Weeks passed and the nights turned so cold that water froze in the bucket inside the cabin. Aspen leaves danced bright yellow. Elk bugled in the meadows. At last the school term was finished and Belle came home. To celebrate her arrival, Eda and Lucy prepared a big dinner of fresh trout, boiled potatoes, and canned corn. Ma unpacked the china and silverware and the best linen tablecloth for the occasion.

"Delicious!" Belle primly dabbed the corners of her mouth with a napkin. "And what lovely flowers. How thoughtful." She examined the bouquet of purple columbine that Eda had picked and arranged in an empty creamed corn can with the label removed.

Eda blushed with pleasure. It seemed to her that Belle had changed, but exactly how she could not say for certain. Perhaps Belle seemed different because she had seen things that Eda had not seen. Maybe she treasured recollections that Eda could not share. She seemed so much older that at first Eda felt shy around her.

"It's a shame your father isn't back in time to enjoy this delightful food," said Ma, who wore her best dress. "I don't know what can be keeping him. He took the pony and said he would be back in a short while. That was hours ago," she said, her face darkening for only a moment. She sipped the tea sweetened with precious sugar that Belle had bought and carried all the way from Cache Creek with the rest of their groceries.

"And to think that Lucy caught the fish. That's the most remarkable thing of all," Belle said. She looked at her sister with a mixture of pleasure and wonder. "How in the world did you ever learn to fish?"

Lucy smiled shyly. "It's not difficult."

"Colorado taught her," Eda volunteered. She took another helping of potatoes, which had taken nearly forever to boil.

Belle appeared confused. "You mean to say that just by being in Colorado she has learned—"

"No, no," Eda said and laughed. "Colorado is a little girl. One of our neighbors."

"She's part of a *mob* of neighbors, to be exact," Ma said and sighed. "Not the best and finest family I've ever met. I've never seen a group eat the way they do. They consume anything that's not nailed down. They're like locusts. Lucy and Eda seem to have made friends with them. Lucy rides over there almost every day."

"Lucy *rides?*" Belle speared a piece of fish with her fork. "Somehow I cannot imagine Lucy galloping around the countryside. Is that wise?"

"She doesn't gallop," Eda corrected her. "And she only rides a little way."

Belle studied Lucy, who squirmed and kept her eyes lowered. "The fresh mountain air seems to be doing you good," Belle said approvingly. "You look strong and healthy. Like a whole new person."

Lucy blushed. "Thank you. You look wonderful too."

Because her two older sisters rarely shared such genuine and kind words of praise, Eda savored the moment. *Perhaps Lucy and I have changed as much as Belle has,* she thought.

"Tell us about Cache Creek," Ma said. "We're eager for news."

"There's not much to tell," Belle replied. "The whole town is just ten or twelve log cabins with a narrow, muddy wagon path that zigs and zags between boulders and tree stumps. On either side of the street stand the stores and businesses—two hotels and one store containing a few yards of calico, some flour, and plenty of whiskey.

"Right now there are nearly one hundred people in town. Almost all of them are miners. Soon everyone will go down to the foot of the mountains. It's too cold to remain in Cache Creek all winter."

"And what about the school?" Eda asked.

"It's in the second floor of the town's tallest building," Belle said. "I taught in a small, narrow room with a low ceiling and two rows of benches.

My table and stool were in the front. We had no books."

"No books?" Lucy asked with surprise.

"None," Belle said and sighed. "The only place to buy books is Denver, one hundred fifty miles away. There isn't any money for that, Mr. Dowdy said. So I had to teach the children what I knew and a bit more that I've heard by word of mouth."

"That sounds difficult," Lucy said.

"Somehow we managed," Belle replied. "One day I had an unexpected visitor from the school board. Mr. Brown unwittingly sat beside a student who kept trying to stick a pin through the poor man's coat sleeve."

"Rude child," Ma said.

"I decided to show Mr. Brown what we'd learned since school began," Belle continued. "Thomas was my brightest scholar. I asked him, 'Who was the first man made by God?' Little Thomas thought for a great long moment, then announced in a loud, proud voice, 'Abraham Lincoln.' You can be sure I dismissed class shortly after that. I was so embarrassed."

They all laughed. Eda felt a genuine sense of relief to see that Belle did not take herself so seriously anymore. How pleasant to joke and laugh together!

Suddenly through the trees came Pa's voice. "Hello? Anyone home?"

Ma and the girls rushed outside in time to see Pa waving his hat and smiling as he walked toward them.

"Pa, where's the pony?" Lucy demanded.

"What kind of greeting for your father is that, my dear?" Ma said. "Mr. Hitchcock, come inside and have some nice supper."

"If you must know, Lucy," Pa said, putting his hand in his pocket, "the pony's right here." When he pulled out his fist and unclenched his fingers, he showed them a small bottle glimmering with three ounces of gold dust.

Eda looked at Pa in disbelief. "You sold him?"

"How could you?" Lucy demanded in a small, sad voice.

Pa's shoulders sagged. "I didn't have any choice. This is the most gold we've seen all summer, right here in my hand," he said in a tired voice. "We're busted. There wasn't enough gold in that claim to fill a thimble."

"Busted?" Ma said the distasteful word incredulously. "You mean . . . you didn't strike it rich?"

"Not the way I promised," Pa said ruefully. "Not the way I planned. Seems like Harry and Dick had the right idea. They lit out yesterday for California."

Eda was stunned. She hadn't even had a chance to say good-bye to Dick and Harry.

"Our only help's deserted us." Ma's face was pale. "What will we do now?"

"Go back," Pa said.

Ma looked at Pa with a confused, miserable expression. "Go back where?"

"Only place we can go. Pennsylvania," Pa said. "I figure if we make it to Denver, we can sell what we don't need. We'll have enough money left to buy food supplies. Then we can head east the fastest, cheapest way possible. We'll use the wagon on the first leg of the journey, then travel third-class train from Quincy to Chicago, Chicago to Cleveland."

"Third class?" Ma muttered. "I refuse to travel third class, Mr. Hitchcock."

"Emily, we don't have much choice," Pa said. "It's third class or walk."

Ma drew herself up very straight. Her face contorted with worry. "How will I ever face Mrs. Osborne again? How will I ever face my sister?

You know how we left, Mr. Hitchcock. It is a terrible humiliation to return even more empty-handed."

Her parents' words buzzed in Eda's head and made no sense. She could not believe what was happening. *Go back?* Two months ago she had wanted nothing more than to see Dragonbreath again, but now, when she thought of leaving Edith and Ulysses and Nebraska and the other children, she felt a terrible ache. *I'll never see them again.*

"We don't have much time," Pa said. "Winter's coming. We have to pack up and get out before the snow falls and drifts too high for us to get through the pass. We'll need every cent we can scrape together, including your salary, Belle."

Belle pursed her lips. "I think it's very unfair that I have to give up all my pay. I worked hard. I was going to buy myself something special."

"Belle, you're being selfish," Lucy announced. "Giving up a little money is nothing. Look what's been taken away from me, something irreplaceable—the pony!" She burst into tears and retreated into the cabin.

"Nothing changes," Belle said with disgust.

"Still the same old Queen Lucy." She marched off to the riverbank to be alone.

"Now look what you've done, Mr. Hitchcock!" Ma exclaimed. "You've ruined our dinner and upset everyone." Ma followed Lucy into the cabin.

Pa shrugged helplessly. "You'd better start packing, Eda," he said and trudged toward the wagon.

Eda stood and watched her family go off in separate directions. She felt like the girl in the parlor lithograph, forsaken and forlorn in a strange place.

September 20, 1864

It is snowing hard and has been for several days and we are making preparations to leave the mountains as there is danger of getting snowed in for the winter if we stay much longer. Last night we were very much disturbed by the howling of wolves.

Pa wrapped the melodeon in canvas and tied it with ropes, then hauled it with great difficulty into the wagon that he had not sold. While Belle and Ma carefully folded clothing and blankets,

Eda took Lucy aside and asked, "Will you come with me to say good-bye to Colorado and the others?"

Lucy shook her head. "I can't walk that far. You say good-bye for me."

"I'm not in a hurry. I'll walk with you, no matter how long it takes."

Lucy seemed determined not to be seen trudging on foot along the path. "I'm not going," she said, sounding vexed. "Don't ask me again."

When Eda arrived at Edith's, the whirlabouts in the yard were strangely silent. It was a windless morning, and she found the lack of usual chaos and noise disconcerting. Where was everyone? She knocked on the door.

"Come in, whoever you are!" Edith shouted.

Eda smiled. Inside the cabin she found the five children squatting on the floor around a spider pan of hot bread and milk. They were busy scooping milk and bread from the three-legged cast-iron skillet. They ate as fast as possible. They did not bother to look up at Eda. At the table sat Edith and Ulysses eating fish and bread.

"Hello, Eda. Care to join us?" Ulysses asked.

"Wyoming, give our guest a hunk of bread," Edith said.

Unwillingly, Wyoming did as he was told. It was not a wise idea to leave the spider even for one moment, as the others quickly began to eat his share of the food. Wyoming tossed the bread in Eda's direction and hurried back to the food on the floor.

"Where's your sister?" Colorado demanded between gulps. "Ain't she coming?"

Eda shook her head. "Pa sold the pony. Lucy didn't think she could walk so far."

Colorado pouted. "She told me she'd come. She promised. I waited a thousand hours."

"She misses you, I know," Eda said, trying to sound reassuring. She nibbled halfheartedly on the hard bread. "I'm afraid we're leaving. Everyone's home packing."

Edith worked a fish bone from her teeth with her finger. "Now, that's bad news. What happened? Did your pa give up?"

"He didn't find any gold," Eda said. "He's afraid we'll be snowed in if we don't leave soon."

"Nine out of ten miners come away poorer than when they set out," Edith said. "It's a great disappointment all the same. Where you headed next? New diggings?"

"We're going back to Pennsylvania," Eda replied.

"That's a long trip," Edith said.

"And plenty of troubles along the way," Ulysses added. "Indians are burning every ranch east of Denver. That's what they say in Fairplay."

Eda couldn't eat any more bread. She held what was left of the chunk in her hand.

"Tsk," Edith clucked. "That might be old news, Ulysses. You needn't scare Eda to death."

"Don't mean to scare her, just to warn her, that's all," Ulysses said.

"You going to eat that?" Wyoming demanded, pointing to the uneaten crust in Eda's hand.

Eda gave him what was left. With difficulty, she cleared her throat. "I brought back the novel you lent me. I wanted to thank you very much."

"I'm glad you enjoyed it," Edith said. She wiped her greasy face with her apron. "We're going to miss you, Eda. You know that. Don't you never give up on your playwriting. I suspect someday to see your name someplace."

Eda nodded. She felt a lump rise in her throat. "I'm going to miss all of you, too. I won't ever forget you." She decided it was better to leave quickly than to linger and have everyone see her cry. She stood up. "My family's probably wondering where I am. I have to go now." But before she reached the door, something grabbed her hard behind her knees and held her legs tight.

"You can't leave till you promise to give this to Lucy," Colorado said. She thrust into Eda's hands a crumpled drawing of a purple pine tree leaning into the wind. An enormous green sun glowed from behind the tree. The picture had been made on the back of an unfolded soap box so that the label was still visible around the edges.

"It's beautiful," Eda said, blinking hard. "The most beautiful tree in the world."

Colorado grinned. "I know. See you later, Alligator."

"After while, Crocodile," Eda said. And she hurried outside. In the yard the metal constructions had begun whirring very slowly, very softly, in the wind. She gave one last look over her shoulder and ran all the way back to their cabin with Colorado's drawing under her arm.

Chapter

10

Not until late that morning were they finally ready to hitch the oxen team and begin the long ride up over the mountain behind the house. "Good-bye, Young America Gulch!" Eda called down into the hollow.

"Adieu!" Lucy and Belle shouted in French. Their voices echoed, *"You . . . you . . . you!"*

Bittersweet sadness pressed between Eda's shoulder blades. Would she ever see this place again? The oxen must have sensed something of the same sentiment. For they too suddenly turned as if to take one last look. When they did so, the wagon overturned. Picture frames, blankets, clothing, and boxes tumbled down the steep incline. The pail filled with milk for their dinner splashed and crashed. And Ma's rocking chair rolled, jumped, and splintered into a million pieces.

"My chair!" moaned Ma. "My best chair!"

"Is everyone all right?" Pa called.

Eda and her sisters were quickly accounted for. Since they were walking, they were not injured— only frightened. "It's a bad omen," Belle mumbled.

"Don't be such a superstitious heathen," Lucy said. "There are no such things as omens."

Belle seemed unconvinced. It took another hour to gather their scattered belongings and repack them before they were ready to go again. "It's a good thing you secured the melodeon with plenty of rope, Mr. Hitchcock," Ma said. "I couldn't bear to lose that, too."

They arrived in deserted Colorado Gulch at dusk. The doors of the deserted and dilapidated buildings creaked idly in the breeze. The heavy snow and gale-force winds of past winters had shifted some of the empty cabins to one side so that they appeared to lounge like picnickers leaning on their elbows against the hillsides. Some cabin walls were decorated with sheets of newspaper, now yellowing and stained and curled. "Pikes Peak or Bust" was scrawled on the wall of one shack. Another visitor had crossed this off and written, "Busted by God."

Pa ignored these signs of failure. That evening he used the lantern to pick through the rocks along the streambed, unable to give up completely on his dream of gold and glory. "It will not hurt," he announced over supper, "for us to stay a few days here for the purpose of prospecting."

Ma fumed. "Is that wise, Mr. Hitchcock? You seem to forget that every day of delay may force us to cross the Great Plains in the dead of winter."

"And what about guerrillas?" Lucy demanded.

"We're completely alone here," Belle agreed. "This is a perfect spot for an Indian ambush."

"Mr. Hitchcock," Ma pleaded, "you said we needed to get out of the mountains as quickly as possible. I think we should keep moving."

Pa flashed a charming smile. "We've come so far, my dear. Wouldn't it be a shame to miss an opportunity that's right before our noses? Who knows what nuggets have been overlooked."

Eda and her sisters sat huddled before the fire. Eda had only one thought now. To go home. But she knew there was no arguing with Pa when he had gold fever.

Oct. 8, 1864

This is a desolate looking place.

Oct. 10

Snow so deep that prospecting is out of question and we started this afternoon on our long journey. Are now camped at the foot of the snow range—

Oct. 11

We crossed the snowy range again. Snow eighteen inches deep. On the top of the range the wind blew very hard and the snow was blowing into drifts. But Pa says "we'll stand the storm it won't be long." We are now camped at the foot of the range in a deserted house. The occupants have been frightened away by Guerrillas.

Two weeks later they descended into lower altitudes and warmer weather and finally arrived in Central City. The enormous quartz mills boomed night and day. Eda held her hands over her ears to keep out the insistent clamor. Naturally, Pa was enthralled by the place, known as "the richest square mile on earth." He went on candlelit tours of mine tunnels to watch buckets of quartz being drawn up out of a shaft 350 feet deep.

Meanwhile, Eda and her sisters marveled at houses that clung precariously to the steep slopes of the gulch like cliff-dwelling birds. The surrounding hills, cleared of timber, were now scarred with stumps, mine shafts, and ore dumps. An acrid cloud of smoke hung over the gulch in the morning. Eda was glad when they finally left.

As they approached Denver one morning, Eda looked down from the foothills and saw the city sprawling below them on the treeless brown plain. Clouds of dust tumbled past, obscuring the view. After months in the remote mountains, Eda felt overwhelmed when she and her family entered the city, only to be swallowed up in noise and confusion and crowds. Brick buildings towered four or five stories high. The wagon and the slow-moving oxen plodded down dust-choked streets laid out on a grid. Fine carriages pulled by spans of fast horses swooped past. Along Cherry Creek, which ran through the town, piles of wood and keeled-over buildings, pieces of furniture, barrels, boxes, and animal carcasses lay in heaps, helter-skelter. The smell was terrible.

"What happened over there?" Eda asked, holding her nose.

"Flood last spring," Pa said. "I heard it came up so fast that no one had time to get out of the way. Twenty people drowned, they say."

Eda and the rest of her family made their way along Denver's busiest street. The bustling crowd included few women. Most of those who roamed the streets were hunters and trappers in buckskin and soldiers wearing gun belts, revolvers, and the big blue cloaks of the Union Army. Tough, dirty teamsters sported leather suits, while horsemen sped by in buffalo-hide boots. Sauntering down the boardwalk were New York dandies in yellow kid gloves and shiny shoes.

"Who are they?" Eda whispered to Pa. She pointed toward a group of men with luxurious mustaches and tall hats, looking proud and proper and very out of place.

"Rich English sporting tourists here to hunt," he replied.

"And look at that!" Ma exclaimed with reverence as they passed an enormous brick mansion in the style of an Italian villa.

Eda stared in wonder at the magnificent lawn. "They even have their own trained deer and dogs."

"They aren't real," Belle said wisely. "They're made of cast iron."

"Oh," said Eda, embarrassed.

To their great disappointment, Pa discovered that the only available housing consisted of two small rooms in a dingy hotel near Cherry Creek. When the wind blew in a certain direction, the smell was horrible. "I'm glad I do not know one soul in Denver. I'd hate to be recognized in such an establishment," Ma grumbled.

While they waited for Pa to lug the heavy valise up the hotel steps, Eda and her sisters peered at a poster hastily tacked to the wall:

ATTENTION, INDIAN FIGHTERS:

Having been authorized by the governor to raise a company of 100 U.S. Volunteer Cavalry for immediate service against hostile Indians, I call upon all who wish to engage in such service to call at my office and enroll their names immediately. Pay and rations same as other U.S. Volunteer Cavalry: salary

40¢ per day. Soldiers entitled to all horses
and plunder taken from Indians.

"This looks serious," Belle said.

"Do you think we are in any danger?" Lucy
wondered. She stood in the shadow of the hotel
doorway, carefully surveying the busy street.
Dust and grit rose in a crazy corkscrew. Newspapers tumbled against the side of the building. "Is
it possible Indians might attack Denver?"

Eda shrugged. She wasn't thinking about their
stay in the city. She was worried about what
might happen when they left Denver and set out
across the open plains.

A leering man and his companion sauntered
past. They smiled at the three girls in a way that
made Belle blush. "Pickpockets, I bet. Better
keep your wits about you. I don't like this place,"
she muttered. "The sooner we leave, the better."

Nervously, Eda surveyed the passing crowd of
strangers. How could she be sure which ones
might slip their hands into her pockets? Maybe
it wasn't safe carrying her precious journal. For
safekeeping, she hid it inside the valise, buried
deep amid their belongings in the wagon. The

valise contained only a few of Belle's dresses. As they had seen scarcely a dozen women since they'd come to Denver, she couldn't imagine that any passing thief would find them of value.

The sky darkened. Pa's face streamed with sweat as he toted a heavy valise up the steps to their rented rooms. Because they were trying to save money for their passage east, they ate a hurried supper while perched on their beds in their two rooms. After she finished eating, Eda felt too tired to do anything except fall into a deep sleep.

The next morning when she awoke, she knew immediately that something was terribly wrong: Ma's sobs from the other room were louder and more exaggerated than any Eda had ever heard before. "You didn't tell me," she wailed. "Why didn't you tell me?"

"I had to sell it," Pa said. He mumbled something. All Eda heard was "We needed the money."

"My melodeon! My precious, dear melodeon."

"And that's not the worst of it," Pa said and lowered his voice. "The sheriff . . ."

Eda strained to hear the rest of what Pa whispered. She could not understand his words.

Suddenly the door slammed. Eda peeked into the other room. Pa was gone.

"We're ruined!" Ma groaned. She buried her face in her pillow.

Nervously, Eda nudged Belle, who was sleeping in the bed beside her. "Are you awake?"

"I am now," Belle grumbled.

"Did you bring in your valise with the dresses last night?"

"It's in the wagon. Don't worry. Pa said it's safe." Belle sat up. Her hair was disheveled. Her worried expression mirrored Eda's. "Why do you ask?"

Eda went into the room where her mother still sat in bed. "There, there," said Lucy, who stood beside Ma, trying to comfort her.

"It's not the end of the world," said Belle, who joined them. "You can always buy a new melodeon when we get back to Pennsylvania. You have to admit it was big and cumbersome and—"

Ma ignored all of them and broke into loud, heartrending sobs. "What will become of us?"

Swiftly Eda wrapped a shawl around her shoulders and tiptoed past her sobbing mother, down the steps to the street. Pa had left the wagon in back of the hotel after unhitching the oxen.

She peered inside, and suddenly she couldn't breathe. She couldn't think. Maybe this was the wrong wagon. Maybe she was mistaken. But the longer she stared, the more certain she became. This *was* her family's wagon.

It was completely empty.

Everything, including her irreplaceable journal, had been stolen.

Chapter

11

During the next three days the temperature plummeted. Snow fell two and a half feet deep. The air was filled with so much white that the nearby mountains seemed to disappear. Wind seeped through the cracks in the hotel wall and shook the dirty windowpane. One morning Eda and her sisters awoke to discover snow blowing across the floor of their rented rooms.

Ma, Eda, and her sisters wrapped blankets around themselves and huddled near the small, coal-burning stove. They were too cold, too miserable, to speak. They simply listened to the wind rattling the window. Eda's stomach growled. She knew their food was nearly gone.

When there was a knock at the door, Eda hurried to open it, hoping that it might be Pa with good news. Instead, she was met by the innkeeper. "I'm sorry," he said, wringing his red hands together, "but I got paying customers wanting to rent these rooms. Now that there are so many paying customers looking for a place to stay in Denver, you folks are going to have to move out."

"That is quite impossible," Ma sputtered indignantly. "It is snowing. We have no money. Where are we to go?"

The innkeeper shrugged. "Tent city."

"Tent *what?*" Ma demanded.

"Many people are trapped here in town because of the bad weather and because the roads are blocked by Indian attack, so the church has set up tents out on the flats. You can stay there free."

"In this weather? I don't think that's wise," Lucy spoke up. "Ma, you know how easily I get sick."

Ma now spoke to the innkeeper in a coaxing voice. "My daughter, sir, is an invalid," she said, pointing at pathetic Lucy who shivered with embarrassment. "As you can see, it is quite impossible for her to go out into this cold climate."

Impatiently, the innkeeper cleared his throat. "You have no money. Your husband told me as much. The tents are free, and they're a sight better than sleeping out in the open."

"Free?" Ma said. "As in charity?" She straightened her shoulders and looked the man straight in the eye with the imperious Derleth glare that had always proved effective back in Erie County. "I will not accept charity. Do you know who I am?"

"Frankly, ma'am, I don't care who you are," the innkeeper replied. "I run a business. I need these rooms. Pack up and be out of here by noon." He turned and left, shutting the door behind him.

Ma's face was pale, drawn. Her lips moved, but no words came from her mouth.

"We'd better get ready to leave," Belle said. She stood up and folded the few blankets they still owned. "Pa will be back soon. Maybe he knows where this tent city's located."

"What's wrong with Ma?" Eda asked.

Their mother sat and stared dully into space. Her shoulders were slumped, her hair disheveled.

"Ma, get up," Lucy insisted. "We've got to pack. We can't stay here."

Still, Ma did not move.

"We'll have to get ready without her," Belle said. "That innkeeper wasn't joking." Reluctantly, the three sisters packed up their few remaining belongings.

When Pa finally returned, the news he brought was not good. The sheriff had been too busy breaking up gunfights and brawls to deal with "another greenhorn's sorry tale of stolen money and goods."

"The thieves are probably headed for Salt Lake City by now," Pa said glumly. "We'll never see that money or our belongings again."

"Including little Colorado's drawing," Lucy said sadly.

Eda clenched her fists in anger. Her journal wasn't worth anything to anyone but her. The person who stole it had probably taken one look at the undecipherable words and dumped it somewhere along the road in the snow, thinking it was just gibberish. She felt furious and helpless. All her most private thoughts, plans, and dreams were gone forever.

"Can't we send a telegram to Uncle Peter asking him to send us money?" Belle asked her father. "He's done it before."

"I don't even have enough money to send a wire," Pa said.

Lucy buried her face in her hands. "We'll never get home again."

"Shut up, Lucy!" Eda shouted. At that moment, if she could have, she would have punched her sister. That was just how frustrated and angry she felt.

"Eda, that's enough," Pa said sternly. "We have to stick together. That's the only way we're going to make it through this."

Eda scowled at her father. *Stick together?* Did Pa know how ridiculous he sounded? This terrible crisis was all his fault. If only he had been more careful and less trusting, he would never have been robbed of all their money. He should have unloaded the wagon completely. They'd still have all their belongings and be on their way at this very moment—not about to freeze to death in some tent in the middle of a snowstorm. With all her might, she grabbed one of their remaining valises, flung open the door, and stomped down the steps as hard as she could.

Late that afternoon in the makeshift tent encampment on the outskirts of Denver, Eda's family crawled inside a battered empty tent. Pa tied down the flapping canvas and shoveled out the snow with his hands. While her sisters perched on boxes and crates out of the wind, Eda left the tent and went exploring.

The snow had stopped falling and she could smell the delicious aroma of pea soup. She followed the scent to its source—a big gray tent where several well-dressed women bundled up in fur hats and mufflers stirred a large kettle. Their long white aprons reminded Eda of the volunteer nurses who helped out at the soldiers' hospital.

"Get away, you!" one of the aproned women shouted to the mob of hungry children who had crept too close.

"Aw, give us a taste!" a boy whined. He hopped back and forth from one rag-wrapped foot to the other as if to keep warm.

"It isn't time yet," the stern-faced woman said. "You know the rules: we ring the bell; then you line up with your bowl."

Eda felt glad to know there would be some hot food for supper that day. She'd have to remember to listen for the bell and be ready with bowls. As she moved on, she saw another blazing fire, this one surrounded mostly by grown-ups. Stones and cast-off bricks had been heaped up to make a low wall inside which a bonfire blazed. Miserable-looking men and women shuffled around the fire. They were bundled up in hats, battered cloaks, blankets, and scarves of every kind.

"Indians. It's all their fault, this trouble we're in. Bloody savages. We should kill every last one of them—man, woman, and child—that's what I say," one man said, rubbing his chapped hands together. His blue cloak was the kind soldiers wore back home.

"Any man who kills a hostile Indian's a patriot," his companion agreed. "I wouldn't have minded joining up with Chivington's Bloodless Third. You get all the plunder and scalps you take. Killing Indians is easy. They ain't human, after all."

"A few months of active extermination against the red devils will bring quiet, and nothing else will," a third man, wrapped up in a buffalo coat, announced in a loud voice.

Blue Cloak spit vehemently into the fire. "I lost everything—my ranch, all my cattle. They burned my place to the ground and scalped my brother just twenty miles from here."

The crowd murmured condolences.

"Me and my family was lucky," Blue Cloak continued. "At least we got away with our lives. Came to Denver for protection. Now look at us. Christmas on the way and me and my children are barely surviving hand to mouth while those red devils laugh and get drunk and live off the government. I tell you," he said, pausing ominously, "I'd kill any Indian I saw, hostile or not."

Eda crept away, confused by what she had seen and heard. Was what they were saying true? If the Indians hadn't been on the warpath, Denver wouldn't have been cut off. As it was, she decided, everything that had happened to them since they came to Denver was the Indians' fault, even the high price of food and the lack of a decent place to live. The family's money and Eda's precious journal would not have been stolen if the Indians had not made the thieves so desperate. Eda hated Indians. They were responsible for ruining everything.

Miserably she shuffled through the snow

toward the nearest building. The sign was covered with a thick layer of snow. She saw people wandering in and out, stamping their feet on the wooden porch before they entered. Thinking it might be warmer inside, she slipped through the door and found herself in a dry goods store. Because she did not want to be accused of loitering with no money to buy anything, she drifted toward the back of the store and pretended to inspect the blankets, ax handles, pails, and buckets displayed along the wall.

All the while she watched the customers waiting in line. Most of them carried buckskin bags with a drawstring tied at the top. Some had little glass bottles hanging around their necks on strings. When they bought supplies from the dwindling goods on the shelves, they reached into their little bags for a pinch of gold dust or shook some out of their little bottles onto a piece of paper on the counter.

"Where's your scale, Ormond?" a heavyset bearded man asked the store owner.

"Broke," beady-eyed Mr. Ormond replied.

"Shot up's more like it," the man murmured. He took three more pinches from his buckskin bag and sprinkled them onto the counter as payment. Each time he did so, Eda noticed that a few grains of gold dust trickled to the floor. Neither Mr. Ormond nor any of the other grown-ups seemed to notice. The customer hoisted the small bag of flour he'd purchased and then stepped right over the grooved floorboards where the gold had landed. With each customer, the routine was the same. Because prices were high, the customers had to pinch repeatedly into their gold pouches.

"Can I help you, gal?" Mr. Ormond said to Eda. "You been standing over there long enough. You going to buy something, or you just trying to get warm? I ain't running no charity house here."

Eda gulped. She studied the gleaming specks caught in the floor cracks. When she looked up, she found herself staring at a row of buckets. "Sir, I just wondered," she said, suddenly inspired, "if you could use some help cleaning up the place. Maybe I could wash your floor."

"Wash the floor?" Mr. Ormond said. He scratched his bald head. "Most children ask me for free candy sticks. They don't ask to wash the floor."

"My family's hard up right now. We could use some money," Eda said, glad Ma wasn't there to hear her.

"Everyone's hard up," Mr. Ormond grumbled. He drummed his fingers on the counter. "You one of the go-backs roosting in the tent city?"

Eda nodded, trying not to feel insulted. "Yes, sir."

"I close up at seven o'clock sharp. You be here and sweep and mop, and I'll give you a nickel's worth of gold dust. How's that?"

Eda sucked in her breath. "All right," she said.

After soup that night in the cold line outside the tent, Eda told Belle that she was going to the dry goods store on a special errand and that Belle was not to tell anyone where she'd gone. "I'll be back as soon as I can," Eda promised.

"What am I supposed to say when Ma and Pa notice you're missing?" Belle demanded.

"Say I went to church. Say I went to visit the sick. Say anything you like," Eda said and hurried away.

After Mr. Ormond closed the store, he gave Eda a broom, a pail, and a mop. "You got any pins?" Eda said innocently.

"Pins? What you need pins for?" he demanded.

"I do a very thorough job," Eda said. "I find pins work best to dig out the dirt in the floorboards."

"Don't take all night, you hear?" Mr. Ormond

said impatiently. With some reluctance he handed her a paper of pins. "Only don't walk out with none of them pins. You got one hour to finish." He took out a cigar. Clearly he meant to relax and smoke while Eda worked.

"Where shall I put the floor dirt when I'm through?"

Mr. Ormond pursed his lips with impatience. "Put it where dirt goes—outside. Child, can't you see that I want to sit down and read my newspaper in peace?"

Eda smiled as she watched him retreat to the back room to smoke his cigar and read the newspaper. She'd take the dirt outside all right.

Eagerly she went to work. She filled the bucket with water and washed the floor thoroughly on her hands and knees, taking special care in the area near the counter. Whenever she rinsed out her rag, dirt and gold flecks floated to the bottom of the bucket.

Eda took the bucket out behind the store. Remembering the way she had helped Pa and the others pan for gold, she carefully rocked the pail and spilled out the water so that only the heavy gold flecks were left at the bottom. Then she poured the remaining water through a sieve she made with the fabric of her apron. To her delight, she discovered several pinches of gold, which she carefully tied in a knot inside her apron.

Back inside, she used a pin to pry some more gold flecks from the cracks in the floor. Eda added these to the apron knot.

"Hour's up. Are you finished?" Mr. Ormond asked.

"Yes, sir. How does it look?" Eda gripped the knotted corner of her apron in one hand.

"Never been so clean in all its days. I'll give you your nickel's worth of dust." He pulled a tiny bottle from his vest pocket. "You got something to carry this in?"

"No, sir," Eda said, holding her apron corner tighter.

Mr. Ormond tapped the few gold flecks into a little empty bottle. "Here . . . that's a nickel's worth. You can keep the bottle if you like."

"Thank you!" Eda said and hurried through the door carrying the dirt outside, just as Mr. Ormond had requested. The greedy merchant would never know that she'd made far more than a nickel washing his floor.

When Eda returned to her family's tent, Pa was angry with her for leaving without telling anyone. He softened considerably as soon as she showed him the gold dust she had brought from her cleaning job at the dry goods store. "Good for you, Eda!" he exclaimed.

"Nice work!" Lucy said. Belle nodded.

"This is enough gold dust for you to send telegrams back to Pennsylvania asking to borrow money," Eda replied in a proud voice. For once she didn't feel like the useless, ignorant youngest child—the one least likely to be of help to anyone. She felt grown up and enormously pleased with herself.

"An excellent suggestion," Pa said. He held the little bottle up so that Ma could see it from where she sat in the corner of the tent. "Look what Eda brought home."

"To think that one of my daughters had to go on bended knee to wash someone's floor," Ma said in a quavering voice. "It is more than I can bear, Mr. Hitchcock."

Pa did not linger to argue with her. Instead he hurried to the nearest telegraph office. While Eda and her sisters waited for his return, they spent their time in the tent describing exactly what they would do once they got home again.

"I'll visit my best friend," Eda said.

Belle looked dreamily at the ceiling. "I'll go to the finest shop on Main Street and buy the biggest, most expensive hat I can find. What about you, Lucy? What's the first thing you'll do?"

"I shall ride in the carriage to our dear old church," Lucy said.

"No doubt to visit the minister," Belle said, stifling a giggle.

Lucy blushed. "To attend services," she said primly.

The girls waited and waited. Finally, when they had almost given up on Pa's return, they heard his footsteps outside the tent. Before he came inside, he shook snow from his coat.

"Did you send the telegram?" Eda demanded.

Pa looked at each girl in turn, his eyes filled with disappointment. "I couldn't send anything."

"Why not?" Belle said.

"Didn't you have enough gold to pay for the telegram?" Lucy asked desperately.

"That's not the problem." Pa shook his head. "Indians have cut the telegraph lines. No word can get in or out of Denver."

Chapter 12

As Christmas approached, Eda felt sadder and more homesick than ever. Back in Erie County, she knew that Dragonbreath was stringing popcorn and cranberries, sledding down the hill, and skating on the pond. Eda closed her eyes and imagined the stockings hanging in the parlor, stuffed to overflowing with oranges and chocolate candies. She could smell the fragrant, brightly lit pine tree. There would be carols and presents and a massive goose for dinner . . .

But not for her. This year there would be no Christmas.

Every day was the same. She and her sisters

shivered in the soup line as they waited for something to be scooped from the bottom of the big sooty kettle. They quickly ate donated bread or stale cake. Then they spent the rest of the day trying to keep warm. On occasion they went to the Presbyterian Sabbath school, if Belle didn't mind being seen in the same dress again and Lucy didn't refuse to walk.

One day, after much persuasion, Belle joined Eda on a rare trip downtown to stare at the Christmas decorations in the shop windows on Denver's busiest street. As they admired hair combs and watch fobs and gold foil Christmas cards, they heard the startling sound of cheerful band music. Next came the roar of cheering, the pounding of horses' hooves, and the loud crack of guns being fired as if in celebration.

A parade of hundreds of soldiers in light blue uniforms marched past in formation. In the lead was a stout bearded man with a determined look. The soldier beside him carried a long pole with a live eagle tied to one end. The troops waved their hats and shouted to the gathering crowd, "Five hundred Indians killed!"

It wasn't long before the crowds along the street began cheering. Some men threw their hats into the air. Others stumbled from saloons brandishing bottles. "Hurrah for the Colorado Third!" they shouted. "Hurrah for Chivington!" Women wept for joy. Children jumped and clapped.

Eda found herself cheering, too. "What does it mean?" she shouted at Lucy.

Lucy, who was busy waving her handkerchief, turned and said, "If so many Indians have been killed, the way east will soon be clear. They'll be able to fix the telegraph line. Then we can get our money from Uncle Peter and go home."

Eda cheered louder. It was a great day. A wonderful day.

"The redskins is whipped!" someone in the crowd screamed.

Eagerly Eda read a newspaper article that one store owner had hastily tacked up inside his display window:

BIG INDIAN FIGHT

The First and Third Regiments have had a battle with the Indians on Sand Creek a short distance northeast of Fort Lyon. Five hundred Indians are reported killed and six hundred horses captured. Bully for the Colorado boys!

For two solid days Denver celebrated. Schools and banks were closed. Politicians gave speeches on street corners. Bands played everywhere. Saloons and restaurants were so jammed with customers that the whiskey supply ran out. Day and night, gunfire and fireworks filled the air as if Christmas and the Fourth of July had been rolled into one holiday.

Colonel Chivington's glorious victory was all anyone spoke of in tent city. How the Fighting Pastor, as he was called, had marched his men 260 miles through deep snow in five days. How the cavalry horses had survived on scant forage and miraculously made their way, although there was no road. How the soldiers had surprised a large, well-armed Indian village. There were a thousand incidents of individual daring. Some said it was the greatest victory over the Indians of all time.

Returning soldiers displayed Indian scalps to prove their bravery. They entertained crowds with stories of how they'd obtained the shriveled bits of skin and scraggly hair that they waved on poles as they paraded wobble-kneed through town. Soldiers with trophies they claimed were Indian ears and noses and fingers and skulls were toasted and given free drinks in saloons. It was a glorious moment for the Bloodless Third Regiment, which had been renamed the Bloody Third in honor of their great accomplishment. The soldiers had liberated Denver, and everyone was grateful.

Somehow the glorious victory made the Christmas celebration in town that much more elaborate. Churches planned free dinners for the many emigrants still stranded in town. Charities planned extensive giveaways. Eda was delighted. Maybe they'd have Christmas after all, now that her family planned to attend the special evening celebration organized by the Presbyterian Sabbath school.

When Belle heard the news, however, she complained, "If only I had something new to wear. I have only one good dress left. All the rest are gone forever."

"Your fancy green silk dress looks fine to me," Eda said. "They're having a real sit-down dinner at church, I've heard. And carols and a Christmas tree."

"The proper way to go to church on Christmas is in a carriage," Lucy pouted. "Since Pa exchanged the wagon and team for food, we'll have to walk. You know how I feel about such humiliation."

"We're all walking together," Eda replied. Then she added in her most pious voice, "It would be a shame if you allowed your pride to keep you from going to our Sunday school celebration and listening to the Reverend Mr. Day speak."

"Well, I . . ."

"I hear he's very handsome," Eda added.

Lucy arched an eyebrow. Without another word, she tied the ribbons of her bonnet under her chin in preparation for leaving.

"Are we ready at last?" Pa said, impatiently tapping his foot.

Ma crossed her arms in front of her. "I've changed my mind. I'm not going."

"Come along," Pa tried to cajole her. "The girls are waiting."

"Do you know what a humiliation it is for me to be seen in public in this dirty old outfit?" Ma hissed. "Do you know what a humiliation it is for me to accept charity like a derelict or a washerwoman?"

Pa sighed. "You can't stay here in this tent alone. There are too many drunk soldiers roaming about. Put your hat on and let's get moving."

"You leave me no choice," Ma said in a pathetic voice. "Oh, my nerves! My poor nerves! It's a good thing Mrs. Osborne can't see me."

The church was packed to overflowing. Eda felt as if all eyes were on her and her family as they walked down the aisle in search of empty seats. She hoped no one would notice that one of her shoes was tied together with string or that her coat sleeve was torn and badly mended. Everyone in the pews looked so fine and clean and well scrubbed.

"I shall die of embarrassment," Ma mumbled and lowered herself into a seat. Across the aisle, a well-fed, neatly coiffed woman in a fashionable satin bonnet leaned forward to inspect Ma and her three ragged daughters. The woman lifted one velvet gloved hand and tittered.

Eda felt her face flush. Back in Pennsylvania, the Derleths had their own special pew in front. Ma and several of her sisters were the ones who donated Christmas gifts to the needy of Erie County. Had they acted as superior as these women? Eda could not remember.

After a long and boring sermon by tall, dark-haired Reverend Day about the victory of the righteous, the choir sang beautiful carols. Candles were lit on the enormous Christmas tree festooned at the front of the church. The church was deliciously warm and fragrant. Eda felt her eyes mist over with sadness and longing. She wondered what Edith and Ulysses and the children were doing at that very moment. Were they having Christmas, too? It was comforting to recall how happy they were with almost no possessions except what they could invent. Why couldn't her family be content with just as little?

Suddenly Eda felt Lucy jabbing her in the ribs with her elbow. "Go on up there. They're asking children to pick a gift from the tree. Belle and I are too old. You go."

"Me?" Eda was so accustomed to thinking of other poor children picking gifts the way they had at home that she had never considered being able to enjoy the same treat. She stood up and shot a quick look at Ma, who averted her eyes, completely humiliated.

"Go on!" Belle prompted. "Pick something nice."

Eda stumbled to the front of the church behind a dirty little boy who smelled strongly of wet wool and urine. She tried not to breathe through her nose. She glanced up at the brilliant tree and was overwhelmed by the possibilities. There were little dolls with shining porcelain faces so high that no one could reach them. Satin pin cushions and toy bugles dangled from branches like heavy fruit, but Eda didn't want any of these things.

She felt someone push her from behind. "Pick, will you? We're all waiting."

Eda scanned the tree and licked her lips. She didn't want to make the wrong choice. This would be her only Christmas present. She tiptoed around the tree. The crowd began to laugh as if amused that she could not decide. "Dear, please hurry," hissed a matronly woman in black brocade. She seemed to be the stern overseer of the distribution of plenty.

Eda searched through the back branches and finally saw the Christmas gift she wanted. "That," she said, pointing to a little cardboard-bound ledger album with a small pencil tied to a purple ribbon. The cover was a marbled green.

The matronly woman clucked her tongue. "You took so long to pick *that?*" she said in an amused voice as if Eda had made a very bad choice. She directed her assistant to unhook the notebook and handed it to Eda.

Eda hugged the gift and hurried back to her pew. There were so many other children waiting in line in restless anticipation for the doll or the jacks or the bright toy trumpet that no one seemed the least bit interested in the notebook that she cradled in her arms.

"Took you long enough," Lucy whispered.

"What is it?" Belle demanded.

When Eda showed her sisters the wonderful little notebook, they looked disappointed. "There were plenty of better presents than that," Lucy said and sniffed.

"How selfish can you be?" Belle complained. "You could have picked a ribbon or a comb and given it to me."

"A notebook?" Lucy said and shook her head. "That was a stupid thing to pick."

But Eda did not think her gift was stupid. The little ledger would take the place of the journal that had been so cruelly stolen. She could hardly wait to open it up and begin writing. When she peeked inside the sweet-smelling blank pages, her heart gave such a leap that she wanted to begin writing immediately.

But when she licked the end of the pencil and was about to put the sharpened end to the beautiful clean paper, Ma gave her such a threatening look that she decided against it. Everyone was bowed in prayer. Eda did the same.

When they emerged from the church, overheated and rosy-cheeked, Eda could hardly wait to get back to the tent where she could examine the beautiful notebook. She tucked it under her arm and leaned over to retie her boot lace. As she did so, her parents and sisters wandered ahead of her.

"Hurry up, slowpoke!" Belle called and soon disappeared in the crowd.

Eda struggled to retie her frayed lace. Someone bumped her. Her notebook flew out from under her arm and landed in the snow. A swift hand grabbed the notebook.

"Give that back!" she screamed.

"Too late, pauper-girl," taunted a big boy in a fine coat with a velvet collar. He had narrow-set green eyes and greasy blond hair combed down over his low forehead.

Eda lunged for the notebook, but the boy was too fast. He dodged out of her way. He darted under a ladder leaning against the church. He tossed the notebook to his friends, who began to play catch. Back and forth, back and forth the notebook flew through the air.

Eda clenched her fists. She bent over and with all her might head-butted the boy with the greasy hair. He fell over into the snow. His friends hooted. "Beat up by a girl, Jamison!"

By this time the crowd of churchgoers had grown too interested for the boys to be able to torture Eda much longer. "Give it back!" she cried.

"Be a gentleman for once, Jamison," a tall man in a top hat told the boy.

Jamison, who seemed to be the man's son, looked at Eda with contempt. "Why should I? She's just a poor ugly girl." He grabbed the notebook from his friend and with one quick movement, flung it onto the church roof.

The man grabbed Jamison by the back of his velvet collar and kept walking until a woman dressed in rustling mauve silk protested shrilly. The man let Jamison go, and he ran away.

Eda crumpled onto the ground. She held her

hands over her face and sobbed inconsolably. She didn't care that the church crowd had to walk around her. She didn't care that people were looking at her and whispering. She had lost her journal. Now she had lost her new notebook as well. She sobbed and sobbed.

"Get up!" Someone roughly took Eda by the arm. It was Belle. "What is wrong with you? Why are you making such a spectacle of yourself?"

Tears streaming down her face, Eda pointed toward the corner of the church roof where the little notebook's pages fluttered in the Christmas wind. "Someone threw my gift up there!"

Belle took one look at the roof. She glanced at the staring, amused faces in the crowd. "It can't be helped," she said. "Next time don't ruin Christmas by picking something that people will make fun of."

Eda burst into fresh tears. *No one understands. No one.*

Chapter 13

That night Eda dreamed of the trapped notebook, its pages flapping sadly like the wings of an injured bird. And then Edith's voice once again reminded her how to walk a tightrope. "Keep your eyes steady," she said cheerfully, "and your body balanced."

When Eda woke up in the darkness, she decided to overcome her fear of heights and climb up on the church roof to fetch the notebook. If it stayed up there much longer, it might be irreparably damaged by snow. But if she retrieved it now, she could dry the pages carefully. A wrinkled notebook was better than none at all. She slipped out of bed, wrapped herself in an extra shawl, and tiptoed out of the tent, her teeth chattering.

Overhead the moon shone in a waning crescent. The streets were dark and abandoned. Thick snow muffled distant voices from the saloons. Instead of feeling frightened, Eda felt strangely powerful. She hurried along the dimly lit street to the church and looked up at the roof. At that moment her courage left her.

In the darkness the tall church seemed to rear up like a startled beast. How would she ever reach the steep roof where the journal fluttered and flapped in the wind? It seemed impossibly high. When she circled the church, she saw a small window near the steeple, but it was covered with bars. Even if she could find some way inside the church, how could she climb out of that window and crawl onto the roof, which was undoubtedly coated with treacherous ice and snow?

Slowly Eda circled the building again. As she did so, she bumped into something. She stopped, stunned. A ladder! Exactly what she needed. With all her might she hoisted the wooden ladder onto her shoulder. It crashed noisily against the building. Eda stopped, terrified that someone might have heard her. Someone might come and arrest her. But no one did. So she kept walking, slowly, carefully. *Keep your eyes steady and your body balanced.* Finally she made her way around to the corner of the building, where she propped the ladder against the wall. Then—quietly, carefully—she began to climb up.

Even though it was cold enough to see her breath, her hands began to sweat. The rungs felt slippery. She gulped for air but did not look down. She kept her eyes straight ahead on the ladder's rungs. Higher, higher she climbed until at last she reached the topmost rung. She reached up as high as she could.

Not high enough.

She tried again, reaching higher. The ladder wobbled. Eda gasped. With outstretched fingers she barely caught a page of the fluttering journal and pulled it toward her. She shifted her weight. The ladder steadied itself. She seized the little book and stuffed it inside her dress. Her heart pounded. *Don't look down.*

Just as she was about to descend, she heard voices below her. She froze, terrified.

"Hurry . . . the key!" a woman said. Her voice was high-pitched, worried. "What if we're seen?"

"Get inside quickly," a man's familiar deep voice said. ". . . promise . . . we won't move." And then he murmured something urgent that Eda could not understand. He seemed to be speaking a different language. The wall the ladder leaned upon shook as the door below her suddenly swung open. She gripped the ladder hard and took one quick look down. A light from inside the church briefly illuminated the figures: two Indian women wrapped in blankets and three smaller children. Nearby stood a tall man and a white woman. The door slammed shut. The light was gone. The vision vanished.

Reverend Day!

Eda could not breathe. She could not think. Why was the minister sneaking Indians into his church? Didn't he know they were the enemy? They'd steal everything; then they would murder him. And that woman—the one with the worried voice—who was she? Another captive? Slowly Eda lowered herself to the ground. She heard no voices coming from inside the church. It was as silent and dark as it had been when she arrived. Eda hid in the shadows. She looked all around her. Reverend Day and the white woman had seemed afraid of being followed. Were there other

Indians out there, waiting? Edna hugged the journal tightly and ran as fast as she could back to the tent.

In the darkness she carefully opened the journal to see if the pages were soggy. But her hands were so cold that she could feel nothing. She wrapped herself in a blanket and slept fitfully until first light.

The next morning Eda could not banish from her mind the image of the minister letting Indians into the church. She knew she couldn't tell her parents. They wouldn't understand, and she'd be in trouble for running off. Had what she had seen been a dream? But the troubled voices had seemed so real. *Promise we won't move.* That was what the Reverend Mr. Day had said. Why? She knew she must find out. What if the pastor was in trouble? What if the Indians were holding *him* captive?

"Where do you think you're going?" Belle demanded when she noticed Eda sneaking out of the tent.

"Come back here, Harriet Adelle," Ma called. "It is far too early for you to be roaming about. We need wood for the camp stove."

Eda retreated into the tent. She had to plan her escape carefully. She and her sisters quickly ate thin, boiled cornmeal without milk or sweetener. Eda knew she would not be allowed to leave unless Lucy or Belle went with her. "The ladies at the Presbyterian Sabbath school have a special sewing project," Eda said to Ma. "They need help. They asked me to come this morning."

"They asked *you?*" Belle said in disbelief.

Eda nodded. She had to think fast. "They said I was a likely candidate for . . . uh, salvation, and the Reverend Day said I should bring my sisters, too."

Belle and Lucy exchanged hopeful glances.

"Did he mention us by name?" Lucy asked.

Eda nodded, secretly amused to see how easily her sisters could be flattered. "He called you by your proper Christian names of course. Hannah Lucille and Sarah Belle."

Lucy and Belle smiled with pleasure.

"Then you must go," Ma said. "Heaven knows it's warmer in the church than it is in this tent."

Lucy clutched her prayer book. Belle took along her sewing kit. She said it made her look industrious and helpful while she listened to a

Bible talk. When no one was looking, Eda tucked
her new journal into her pocket for safekeeping.

She hurried with her excited sisters to the
church. They knocked. No one answered. "Are
you sure the Reverend Day said today?" Lucy
demanded.

Eda nodded. She knocked harder. What if she
was too late? What if the Indians had already
done their dirty deed and escaped?

Suddenly the door opened a crack. The same
woman's voice from the night before whispered
urgently, "Yes? What do you want?"

"We've . . . we've come," Eda stammered, "to
help."

"Did Mr. Day send you?" the woman hissed.

"Yes," Lucy and Belle chimed in.

"Did anyone follow you?" the woman
demanded.

"No," Eda said. *What a strange question.*

The door opened wider. The woman, who was
dressed in dull purple, wore her dark hair pulled
back in a severe bun. She quickly glanced up and
down the street and ushered Eda and her sisters
inside the church. Then she locked the door behind them. "Good. I'm glad you brought your
sewing supplies. Follow me," she said. She spoke

in a friendly but businesslike tone, as if she knew exactly who they were.

Belle and Lucy seemed disturbed by the locked door and the odd questions, but they did as they were told. Eda and her sisters followed the woman through another door, which she locked behind them with another key. They hurried down a long hallway to still another door, which also had to be unlocked. Finally they came to a small room that appeared to be in the cellar of the church. There were no windows and only one lantern. Eda held her breath, certain that she and her sisters would find the poor minister being held captive. *We should have brought a weapon,* she thought. She looked nervously about, suddenly aware that she had never thought of an escape plan.

"Over here, please," the woman said. She led the girls through another doorway and up a flight of narrow dark steps. And in this room, which was small but lit by one window, Eda saw three young Indian girls and two older women cowering in the corner. Immediately, Belle and Lucy stopped in the doorway and refused to walk any closer.

The Indian girls hid their faces and turned

away. The two women looked at Eda and her sisters with fierce expressions.

The woman in the purple dress said something to the Indian women in a strange language that Eda could not understand. The women did not respond. They sat on the floor, immovable, in front of the children. Their buckskin and gingham dresses were filthy. Their lank, greasy braids hung over their shoulders. One woman's arm was wrapped in a dirty rag that was stiff with dried blood. The women's legs were scarred, their moccasins nearly shredded.

"My name is Amelia Lambert," the woman in purple said. "Please hang your wraps on those hooks." She pointed to the hooks on the walls. On a nearby table were two bolts of hideous cheap fabric, a pot of tea, several dirty cups, and a plate with several partly eaten crusts of bread. "We do not have much time. Reverend Day wants us to sew some new clothing for the little girls before they are sent away to the States to be educated. I confess it would be best for them to be washed and scrubbed thoroughly but they will not allow any of us to touch them, and of course I understand why, seeing what they have just been through."

Lucy slowly unfolded the coarse red gingham material and looked at it critically. "Miss Lambert, we will have to measure them to make them new dresses."

"Quite impossible," Miss Lambert replied. "They won't let us near them."

"Why?" Eda asked boldly. "Who are they? What are they doing here?"

"You mean Reverend Day hasn't told you? Well, I suppose it's too dangerous. You must promise not to tell a soul. Not even your parents. Do you understand?"

Eda and her sisters nodded.

"They are Cheyenne from Sand Creek," Miss Lambert said, lowering herself slowly onto a chair. "They're the lucky ones. The survivors."

Eda looked with shocked curiosity at the girls, who seemed to be several years younger than she was. This was the closest she had ever been to Indians. They did not seem like vicious, bloodthirsty enemies. They did not seem lucky either. The three little girls looked exhausted and terrified. "Ma'am," Eda asked slowly, "what do you mean, 'survivors'?"

For the first time, Eda noticed how careworn Miss Lambert's face was. She had circles under her eyes and a nervous tremor in her right hand. "On November 29, as you have probably heard, Colonel Chivington and his soldiers attacked a peaceful Indian village of about one hundred thirty lodges. Of the one thousand inhabitants, approximately two-thirds were women and children."

"Was that the big fight everyone's been celebrating?" Belle asked.

Miss Lambert nodded wearily. "Of the two hundred dead, we have been informed by reliable sources that most were women and children, even babies. They were brutally killed—scalped, mutilated. These three little girls and the two women hid under buffalo robes when the soldiers came to burn their village on the second day. Luckily, the men who found them weren't as bloodthirsty as the others. They were protected and brought to Fort Lyon on December 10 and smuggled at great personal risk to this church where their presence must remain secret. I need not tell you why. You have seen what the soldier mobs in Denver have been doing for the past weeks."

Eda thought of the shriveled scalps on display. She looked at the little girl who cried and rocked back and forth on her haunches. "You mean,"

Eda whispered, "everything they've been saying in the newspapers and the speeches is a lie?"

"Everything," Miss Lambert replied in a steely voice. "Of course, when the press back east hears from me and the other witnesses, we hope to alert a Congressional investigation. This kind of whole-sale slaughter of innocent women and children cannot go unpunished."

Eda and her sisters stood awkwardly watching the oldest girl soothe the youngest one. Miss Lambert spoke to her in their language. The sobbing girl muttered a few words and wiped her nose with the back of her hand.

"'Pony-soldiers' is all she ever says," Miss Lambert explained. She rose slowly to her feet and began laying out the fabric. "Will you help us?"

Belle and Lucy nodded. They seemed too stunned to speak. Eda did not know what to say either. What Miss Lambert had told them was an awful, grown-up truth—the kind that Eda's family always avoided mentioning. Clearly, Miss Lambert didn't think Eda was too young or too ignorant to understand what had happened. "What can I do?" Eda asked, determined never again to be a helpless, blundering child with a brat-baby heart.

"You can begin by marking out dress pieces using this pattern," Miss Lambert said. Eda did as she was told. Her sisters cut the pieces from the fabric with scissors.

Another group of assistants arrived. Two more women with more inexpensive fabric and sewing shears, needles, and thread busily went to work with Eda and her sisters. They, too, informed Miss Lambert that they had been sent by Reverend Day.

For hours Eda and the other women cut and stitched. The Cheyenne girls stayed as far away from them as they could. Occasionally they nibbled on some fresh cheese and bread that Miss Lambert brought for them on a tray. But they refused to sit in chairs, and they refused to wash their hands.

Eda, never a very dedicated seamstress, stood up and stretched. Her shoulders ached. She wandered over to the window and looked out at the street. How strange everything must look to the Cheyenne girls. A place so foreign and filled with people who reminded them of the pony-soldiers they feared so much. Eda sat on a box near the little girls and took out her Christmas notebook. Some of the pages were still somewhat damp. She waved the notebook in the air. As she did, she noticed that one of the Cheyenne girls watched her very carefully. She seemed to be perhaps Wyoming's age, maybe eight or nine years of age.

Eda blew on the first notebook page. The girl scooted closer. Eda licked the end of her pencil. The girl came closer still. Eda pretended not to see her. She wrote:

And as thought is ever busy I will make my hands help a little by scratching them down on this new paper, for my diary is too small for the purpose and my memory too short.

The girl watched with rapt curiosity. Eda turned and handed her the pencil and the journal. The girl took them without looking at Eda. She sat cross-legged on the floor and began drawing. She drew what appeared to be a wigwam with a crescent moon on it. A tall woman with long braids stood in the doorway. Again and again the girl drew sharp scratch marks on the wigwam until the page was nearly black. The soft paper began to tear, but the girl kept drawing.

"She's ruining your Christmas present," Lucy said in a critical voice.

"No, she's not," Eda replied softly. "She's showing me how her mother died."

Abruptly the drawing seemed to be finished. The girl turned the page. She began a new picture. And then another. And another. Some were strange horned animals with bright wings. Others were wagons bursting into flames. Bullets and cannonballs suddenly pierced the air. As Eda watched her work, she could imagine the acrid smell of smoke everywhere, the screaming and wailing, the terrible explosions and cries for help. The girl did not say one word to her. Yet Eda knew. She could see from the drawings how the ponies stampeded and the dogs ran wild. How the pony-soldiers with long knives danced in stolen feathers and beads and beat sacred drums. And when the killing was finished, how the coyotes sniffed the dead, who were heaped everywhere.

The girl shut the notebook. She handed it to Eda and for the first time, looked her in the eye. Her glance was plaintive, yet she did not speak. At that moment, Eda understood how alike they were. In the past she had thought all Indians were faceless, nameless enemies. How was she to know that sitting before her would be someone just like her? Someone desperately trying to record what she remembered—what she heard and saw and felt.

"No, you keep it." Eda shook her head and motioned with her hand. "The notebook is for you."

The girl did not look at Eda again. She did not smile. She simply took Eda's Christmas present back to her corner and hid it carefully under a bundle of blankets.

Exactly as Eda would have done.

That evening when Eda and her sisters returned to their tent, they felt weary yet strangely happy. The first thing Belle did was to dig through their battered valise to find her best dress of fine pale green silk. It was all that remained of her luxurious wardrobe.

"What are you doing with those scissors?" Ma cried.

"Making some alterations," Belle said happily. "You'll help me, won't you, Lucy?"

"Certainly," Lucy replied. She winked at Eda.

Together the three sisters snipped and stitched until late into the evening.

"That is far too small for any of you to wear," Ma said critically. "Whatever possessed you to ruin a perfectly good dress? I thought it was your favorite, Belle."

"It *is* my favorite," Belle said. "And it's not ruined, Ma. It's improved. Look, now it has a little apron, too, thanks to Eda."

Eda gaily stood up, holding the apron before her. She made a little curtsy. Her sisters laughed. Lucy wrapped a shawl around her shoulders.

"And where do you think you're going?" Ma said with alarm.

"We're in a bit of a hurry, Ma. We'll explain everything when we get back," Lucy replied. "Come along, Belle and Eda." Lucy carefully rolled the new silk dress and apron into a neat bundle. Her sisters quickly followed her out into the snowy streets.

"What if we're too late?" Eda said. She spotted the church in the distance. Sleigh bells jangled. "There's a light coming from the back. They're leaving!"

As they rushed closer, Eda could make out a group of people draped in blankets being helped into a sleigh. "Wait!" cried Lucy. She bolted ahead, running faster than Eda had ever seen her move in her life.

Miss Lambert, who held the lantern aloft in the sleigh beside the driver, turned when she heard Lucy's voice. The driver reined in the prancing horses.

Lucy thrust the garment into the arms of one of the little Cheyenne girls. "This is a pretty dress we made for you," Lucy said breathlessly.

The girl held the soft material to her cheek and closed her eyes. Suddenly the lantern was extinguished, the driver cracked his whip, the horses leaped forward, and the runners sliced through the snow as the sleigh vanished into the night.

Eda, Belle, and Lucy listened until they could no longer hear the faint music of harness bells. Snow shimmered. Overhead a new moon shone like a promise. "We'd better go back," Eda said, grateful for their incredible good fortune. In spite of everything that had happened to them, they still had each other. That was all that really mattered. She linked arms comfortably with her sisters, one on either side, and together they made their way through the deserted Denver streets.

Epilogue

On January 14, 1865, Eda and her family finally left Denver with borrowed money and began their journey back to Pennsylvania as part of a well-armed wagon train consisting of 150 wagons and 600 men. The military escort included artillery and cannon. The wagon train moved swiftly across the frozen plains, past several smoldering ranches destroyed by Cheyenne and Arapaho in revenge for what would later be called the Sand Creek Massacre.

Their wagon train, however, was not attacked. Eda celebrated her fourteenth birthday on January 25, 1865, "riding all day in the cold," as she laconically wrote. She and her family made it safely across the ice-bound Missouri River, then on through Des Moines into eastern Iowa, where they boarded a train for home.

Author's Note

This book is based on the 1864 journey to the Pikes Peak region in Colorado Territory taken by Harriet Adelle Hitchcock and her family. Two diaries were later discovered, both presumed to have been written by Eda, as she was called by her family. One was brief and unemotional, containing the names of places the family passed through on the first thousand miles of their travels. Sometimes only one word appeared in an entry to describe the weather: "Pleasant." The other notebook was much more intimate and revealed Eda's spunky personality. In an early entry she vowed, "No one will ever see it."

Eda and her sisters were among a small, brave group who assisted a handful of survivors of the Sand Creek Massacre, a fact never reported by the *Rocky Mountain News* or other early annals of Denver's history. After the incident on Sand Creek, word quickly reached Washington, D.C. Although the country was still emmeshed in the tumult of the last tragic months of the Civil War, there was a public outcry against the action taken by Colonel J. J. Chivington and his men, who were accused of numerous atrocities.

On February 1, 1865, a thorough investigation was made of Chivington and his regiment by the U.S. Army. A month later the House of Representatives began hearing testimony from soldiers and other witnesses. Congress compiled a report entitled "Massacre of Cheyenne Indians." Chivington's dream of a brilliant career in politics ended swiftly.

Meanwhile, in the early spring of 1865, the Hitchcock family made the last leg of the journey back to their native Pennsylvania. En route, they passed through Pittsfield and stopped at a relative's home during maple sugar season. Here, Eda met fifteen-year-old Oramel William Lucas, who was helping boil maple sap into sweet, fragrant syrup. Lucas later wrote of that fateful day: "A batch of syrup fresh from sugar bush [a grove of sugar maple trees] was at hand. This was put in the big brass kettle in the fireplace and sugared off. The youngest of our visitors, a girl about my age, and myself with others were helped to hot sugar and we gravitated to the lounge in the corner and chatted as we ate our sugar. It was literally a sweet time and thus began a friendship which eventuated in marriage."

Before she was married, however, Eda would attend Oberlin College in Oberlin, Ohio. Her wedding took place in 1883, when she was thirty-two years old. Eda spent most of the rest of her life with Lucas, who became a Congregational minister, serving in various churches throughout the West. They had one daughter, Ethel Eudora, and a son, Arthur LeRoy, who lived only two years.

Bibliography

PRIMARY SOURCES

Holmes, Kenneth L., editor. *Covered Wagon Women,* Vol. 8. "Thoughts by the Way, 1864–1865," by Harriet Hitchcock. Glendale, Calif.: Arthur H. Clark, 1984.

Sanford, Mollie Dorsey. *The Journal of Mollie Dorsey Sanford in Nebraska and Colorado Territories, 1857–1866.* Lincoln: University of Nebraska Press, 1959.

U.S. Congress, 38th Congress, Second Session, Joint Special Committee to Inquire into Conditions of the Indian Tribes. Appointed under

Joint Resolution of March 3, 1865, reported with Appendix. Washington, D.C.: 1867.

SECONDARY SOURCES

Bird, Isabella. *A Lady's Life in the Rocky Mountains.* Norman: University of Oklahoma Press, 1960.

Black, Robert C. *Island in the Rockies.* Granby, Colo.: Grand County Pioneer Society, 1969.

Conner, Daniel Ellis. *A Confederate in the Colorado Gold Fields.* Norman: University of Oklahoma Press, 1970.

Dallas, Sandra. *Colorado Ghost Towns and Mining Camps.* Norman: University of Oklahoma Press, 1985.

Hedges, William Hawkins. *Pikes Peak or Busted!* Evanston, Ill.: Branding Iron Press, 1954.

Hoig, Stan. *The Sand Creek Massacre.* Norman: University of Oklahoma Press, 1961.

Howbert, Irving. *Memories of a Lifetime in the Pikes Peak Region.* New York: Putnam, 1925.

Jones-Eddy, Julie. *Homesteading Women: An Oral History of Colorado, 1890–1950.* New York: Twayne, 1992.

Lavender, David. *The Rockies.* New York: Harper & Row, 1968.

Mangan, Terry William. *Colorado on Glass: Colorado's*

First Half Century As Seen by the Camera. Silverton, Colo.: Sundance, 1975.

Morgan, Ted. *A Shovel of Stars: The Making of the American West, 1800 to the Present*. New York: Simon & Schuster, 1995.

Paul, Rodman Wilson. *Mining Frontiers of the Far West, 1848–1880*. New York: Holt, Rinehart & Winston, 1963.

Rinehart, Frederick R., editor. *Chronicles of Colorado*. Niwot, Colo.: Roberts Rinheart, 1993.

Schenck, Annie B. "Camping Vacation, 1871." *Colorado Magazine*, Summer 1965.

Sutherland, Daniel E. *The Expansion of Everyday Life: 1860–1876*. New York: Harper & Row, 1989.

Svaldi, David. *Sand Creek and the Rhetoric of Extermination: A Case Study in Indian-White Relations*. Lanham, Md.: University Press of America, 1989.

Utley, Robert M. *The Indian Frontier of the American West, 1846–1890*. Albuquerque: University of New Mexico Press, 1984.

Villard, Henry. *The Past and Present of the Pikes Peak Gold Regions*. Princeton, N.J.: Princeton University Press, 1932.

Werstein, Irving. *Massacre at Sand Creek*. New York: Scribner's, 1963.

Writers' Program, Works Projects Administration. *The WPA Guide to 1930s Colorado*. Lawrence: University Press of Kansas, 1987.

About the Author

Trained as a journalist, Laurie Lawlor worked for many years as a freelance writer and editor before devoting herself full-time to the creation of children's books. She enjoys many speaking engagements at schools and libraries, and her books have been nominated for many awards. She lives in Evanston, Illinois, with her husband, son, daughter, and two large Labrador retrievers. Her books include the *Addie Across the Prairie* series, the *Heartland* series, *How to Survive Third Grade*, *The Worm Club*, *Gold in the Hills*, and *Little Women* (a movie novelization). Her nonfiction work, *Shadow Catcher: The Life and Work of Edward S. Curtis*, won the Carl Sandburg Award for nonfiction (1995) and the Golden Kite Honor Book Award (1995).

Turn the page for a preview of
the next American Sisters paperback
Down the Río Grande, 1829
by Laurie Lawlor

Available in November!

The pale, cloudless August sky shimmered with heat. No one in Guerrero could remember a spring and summer with so little rain. Not one drop. Corn had shriveled. The constant east wind scoured across the plains of mesquite and cactus and sang laments among the rows of rattling bean plants struggling to survive along the banks of the shrinking Río Salado, a tributary of the brave, wild river they called Río Bravo.

Dust rose in blinding gusts from nearby low hills. The wind did not discriminate among the poor or the rich of Guerrero. Grit seeped through the open windows and coated the *frijoles* and tortillas, the refried beans and flat corn bread, of families who crowded into the simple huts thatched with willow branches and mud called *jacales*. Grit seeped under the stout oak doors with iron grillwork and massive iron locks of the stone houses and coated the flavored young goat meat dinners of the well-to-do families. Every morning poor and rich alike awoke exhausted and sweaty with their faces powdered in strange patterns and their teeth gray. No one could escape the wind, the dirt, the heat.

As they did every day during the most oppressive, breathless hours of sunlight, the people of Guerrero were taking their siestas. They shuttered their windows with carved wooden panels hung from leather hinges. They closed their small shops. No vendor wandered among the streets calling, *"¡Arroz con leche! ¡Arroz con leche!"* No shouting, barefoot children chased one another in the plaza. All was silent. Even stray dogs crawled into whatever shade they could find. Everyone slept or rested.

Everyone except Rosita.

As silently as she could, she slipped out the door of her father's grand house with the snail carved over the stone portico. She wrapped her white cotton shawl over her head and bare arms. Carefully, she gathered a bundle of her most precious belongings, stuffed them inside a woven *morrales*, and hurried away from her napping family, snoring don Cassos, and the servants who were leaning against the cool stone wall or stretched out on a hard wooden bench in the kitchen. For once she felt free of the prying stares that seemed to follow her everywhere.

There was something different about Rosita. Anyone in Guerrero could see that. Her passing made very old men stop and stare and wish they were young. Very young men stopped and stared and wished they were older. When Rosita walked down the street, dogs looked up from the cool shadows of buildings. Shutters opened. Women raised their hands to their mouths and spoke to each other in lowered voices. In the little village there was no need of wind with so many whispers.

But this time, no one was awake. No one saw her. No one whispered. Without looking back she left the village's blinding white buildings and empty straight streets. The farther from town she traveled, the happier she felt. By the time she headed east past the rocks and falls and reached the barren hills of Río Salado, the invisible burden she carried always on her shoulders seemed to lighten ever so slightly. She could almost breathe freely.

Steadily she walked—not too fast, not too

slow. And whenever she could, she slipped into the shade of a scrubby cactus and waited for her heart to stop beating so hard, for her feet to cool. She held the *morrales* close against herself so that the bulky bag and the front of her dress were wet with perspiration. Even though she wore leather huaraches, she felt the burning ground sear through the thick soles. Her nostrils filled with the herby sweetness of mesquite and the smokey smell of dried creosote and the rich, muddy breath of the river.

She paused to remove a sharp pebble from her sandal.

Just then something crackled. A footstep?

She froze, terrified someone might be following her. There were bandits along the river. And the Comanche were always on the lookout for unwary travelers. Along the road to Dolores, Papa told her of white crosses, the eyes of God he called them, that marked the places where the unfortunate had been robbed and killed.

Rosita took a deep breath. Turning slowly, she caught a glimpse of a brown shape slither under a rock.

Rattlesnake.

She made the sign of the cross and kept moving, careful to keep her distance. Perhaps it was too hot even for an angry rattlesnake.

She hurried on, faster now. Nearby she smelled the strong rotten-egg odor of two sulphur springs where hot underground water boiled and bubbled. Her aunt, dear Tía Lupe, who knew so much about so many things, once told her of the power of these strange gurgling places to heal aching bones and broken hearts. *Ah, poor Tía Lupe! If only these springs had the power to bring you back.*

It was Tía Lupe who had told her after her father had remarried how she should love her stepsisters. How she should cherish them. She spoke of Rosita's mother, her sister, with such tenderness. She called her her history. "We were partners in time. Fellow travelers. Witnesses," she said. But Rosita could never imagine being a fellow traveler with either Frida or María. She was glad to leave Guerrero and journey far away. She didn't care if she ever saw her stepsisters again.

Rosita walked on and on. In the distance she heard the current, the ebb and crash and ripple of moving water and saw the silver thread, the path the Río Bravo took. She hurried faster. She could smell the river—stronger now. The scent of exotic and faraway places the river had traveled. Somewhere far to the north, she had been told, were impossibly steep, snow-covered mountains that were the source of the Río Bravo. And many leagues to the south the river emptied into the ocean. Papa said the ocean was not like the river. It tasted salty and stretched so wide that sailors who were brave enough to travel far enough could look in all directions and see no land— just open water and glinting sunlight. What kind of freedom would that be?

Gathering the shawl around her head and shoulders to shield her from the sun's glare, she searched up and down the river. This bend was the place she had been told the steamboat was moored.

But she saw nothing.

Her shoulders sagged. She was too late. The boat was gone. The muddy current swirled and rippled. It crashed and gurgled and cascaded. Her mouth filled with the taste of bitterness. She hugged her bundle tight and listened to the river mock her.

"Rosita!"

Instantly, Rosita crouched low on the ground beside a boulder. *María!* Always following her everywhere like a shadow. Ruining everything.

"Rosita?"

Rosita bit her lip to keep from shouting in anger at her annoying stepsister. *Go away!*

"Rosita, where are you?"

Now her stepsister's voice sounded frightened. Rosita smiled. *Serves you right.* She tried to make herself smaller. Perhaps if she remained perfectly still, timid María would give up and go home—back to her books. She wouldn't have to talk to her. She wouldn't have to explain what she was doing here.

The wind chanted and the river crashed and rumbled past. Rosita strained her ears in hopes of hearing María's footsteps becoming fainter and fainter, moving away from her. But she heard nothing. Rosita scowled. *Did she fall in the water?* Rosita knew her ill-tempered stepmother would never forgive her. María could not swim. If she drowned, it would be Rosita's fault. That was what her stepmother would say. "You are cursed like all the women in your family."

Rosita hesitated. She listened for the sound of a cry, a splash. And when she could wait and listen no longer, she stood up and shouted, "María?"

"Yes?"

There was María, perched on a nearby rock, grinning like a fool. For once she carried no books. Her coarse black hair was tangled around her sweaty face. She had ripped her long skirt. And she wore nothing to protect her head. Perhaps the sun had made her *loca*.

"Why do you follow me like this?" Rosita demanded furiously. "Leave me alone."

"I thought you'd be glad to see me," María said. Her smile vanished. "What is that you're carrying?"

"Nothing," Rosita replied. She tucked the bundle behind her back. "Does your mother know where you are?"

María shook her head shyly. "I know how to be silent, too. You thought I was sleeping, didn't you? Maybe you'd like some company. That's why I followed you."

"Company?" Rosita exploded. She tilted her head back, opened her mouth, and laughed. Her loud donkey laughter echoed along the river. "Whatever made you think that?"

María looked at her dirty feet and shrugged.

When Rosita saw her stepsister's sad expression, she stopped laughing. "I am sorry. I didn't mean to insult you. Sometimes I just say things that get me into trouble. Are you all right? Maybe too much sun. Sit over here." Rosita pointed to a small patch of shade beside some mesquite. If María collapsed from sun sickness, how would she ever carry her back to the village? Luckily, she had a few *chié* in her pocket and a hollow gourd that she had intended to use on her journey. "I'll mix you something to drink to bring you back to your senses."

María did as she was told. She watched Rosita scoop up some river water and carefully drop in the seeds.

Rosita swirled the mixture. In seconds, the water in the gourd began to thicken. "Here now, take a sip. Only one. Slowly, foolish one. Don't spill it."

María took a sip and made a face. "Tastes like spit."

"Too bad. You'll drink some more in another minute."

María sighed. Quietly she asked, "Why don't you help anyone else?"

"What do you mean?"

"People come to the house sometimes. Poor people. Women mostly. They say your mother was a skilled *curandera*. But when they ask for herbs and teas that you must surely have learned to make from such an accomplished healer, you refuse. Why?"

Rosita scowled. "It is none of your business."

"It is a gift," María persisted in a timid voice.

Rosita tucked her bundle under her arm. "What do you know of gifts? What do you know of anything? I have my reasons. I do not have to share them with anyone as foolish and rude as you. Drink the rest of this. It's time to go back." Abruptly, Rosita motioned for María to stand and follow her up the hill to the path that led back to Guerrero.

María did not budge. "I am sorry I insulted you. Let me make amends. May I sing you a song?"

Rosita impatiently scanned the river. *"Sí,"* she said, nodding.

"I'll sing one of the *enlaces.* I plan to perform this song of congratulations for your wedding."

"If you like," Rosita said. She could not hide the dread in her voice. *My wedding.* Now that the boat was gone, how would she ever escape?

María's pure, shining voice cut through the hot air like a knife as she sang *"La Pastora":*

> *"A orillas de un sesteadero*
> *una oveja me faltó,*
> *y una joven blanca y bella*
> *de un pastor se enamoró."*

While she sang about a pretty maiden who fell in love with a shepherd boy, Rosita forgot about escape. She simply enjoyed the tune. When María finished, Rosita applauded. "You have a beautiful voice. You should sing loud about daring adventure and heroes so that the whole world can hear you."

María blushed. "I have made up such exciting ballads myself. But you know *corridos* are forbidden to be sung except by men. I would be punished." Whenever she sang at home and sounded the least bit too exuberant, her mother would cover her ears with her soft hands and cry, "*¡Respeto!*" to warn her to keep her tone of respect and sing only in a soft voice—or not at all.

"It's a pity," Rosita replied and began trudging along the path toward the village. María walked beside her. "Why do they say that women are not supposed to sing men's songs?"

María wiped sweat from her forehead. "There are rules. How to wear your *rebozo* to enhance your dignity. How to wear your *rebozo* to carry your baby. How to walk through the village. How to speak to your elders. There are rules, you know. Rules for everything." She paused. "What exactly were you doing here by yourself? Mama says there are bandits along the river. And Comanche. And wild animals. This is no place for you. Why did you come here?"

Rosita felt her face flush with anger. Such an annoying, dull, plodding girl! Always following her like a shadow. Always reminding her of irritating regulations and traditions. If only Papa had never married doña Álvarez. Life would be different. She would have no stepsisters to plague her. "I don't have to tell you anything," Rosita said with a cold, stony expression. "You are not my real sister. You are nothing. You are—"

Suddenly, María gripped Rosita's arm very tightly.

"Let go!" Rosita wriggled free.

María's lips quivered. She pointed with a trembling hand. "Look," she whispered.

Along the bank of the river a coyote with strange yellow eyes watched them carefully. The tangle of dusty mesquite and other low scrub nearly hid the trickster's dun-colored back, its bushy tail and snub snout. The coyote did not waver. It stood its ground and stared.

And in that moment Rosita knew that she and the coyote carried pictures of each other inside their heads. They had met once before beneath the Sangre de Cristo peaks far to the north when their world had been all fur and fang.

"I am going home," María said fearfully. She fled as fast as she could back to the village.

Rosita did not run. Instead she turned for one last look. The coyote had vanished. Rosita quickly retraced her steps back to the river. She searched the riverbank. She was too late again. The coyote was gone.

Just as she was about to walk back to the village, she heard an eerie moaning and saw something coming around the bend. The noise took her breath away.

The great steamboat!

Part winged, part floating creature, the steamboat was as white and gleaming as a dream. It had two enormous wheels turning on either side like strange, splashing wings that scooped up water. Its single, tall black chimney spit black soot, smoke, and sparks. The boat shrieked, splitting the brilliant air. When she heard the high, lonesome call of the steamboat, she heard her mother calling, "Flee, Rosita! Flee!"

In a flash, she dove behind a mesquite bush and quickly opened her bundle. She slipped her expensive, hateful, white wedding dress over her head. She clasped her mother's necklace around her neck and her silk shawl over her shoulders. As fast as she could, she stuffed her other clothing into the bag. Without even stopping to think, without even stopping to breathe, she stumbled down to the shore of the river and waved with all her might.

The boat shrieked again. Were her eyes betraying her? It looked as if it were moving down river. The boat was leaving. Rosita waved her shawl over her head. "Stop!" she screamed. "Take me with you!"

The boat gave another terrible howl. A man with bright red hair the color of fire stepped to the top of the boat. He waved back. His face was shockingly pale. Was this the great Señor Austin?

She waved again.

This time she could not believe her eyes. The steamboat stopped. Another smaller boat was lowered into the water. A man rowed toward her. Unlike the man with the hair the color of fire, this large man was very black. The color of smoke. Rosita felt frozen to the spot.

For the first time she had doubts. *Maybe running away is a mistake.* Maybe she should not go near anything so powerful and mysterious.

Only when the black man smiled and waved, speaking broken Spanish in greeting and gesturing in a friendly way, only then did Rosita break out of her trance. She took one swift look over her shoulder and climbed unsteadily into the little boat.